WELCOME TO SEABURY

SEABURY - BOOK 1

BETH RAIN

Copyright © 2021 by Beth Rain

Welcome to Seabury (Seabury: Book 1)

First Publication: 30th July, 2021

All rights reserved.

No part of this book may be reproduced in any form or by any electronic or mechanical means, including information storage and retrieval systems. Except for use in any review, the reproduction or utilization of this work, in whole or in part, in any form by any electronic, mechanical or other means now known or hereafter invented, is forbidden without the written permission of the publisher.

Published by Beth Rain. The author may be contacted by email on bethrainauthor@gmail.com

❊ Created with Vellum

CHAPTER 1

Kate Hardy let her eyes rest on the horizon as the sound of the waves washed over her. She knew she really should get up from her grassy perch next to the old lighthouse and get back to the café, but she couldn't resist a couple more minutes in her favourite place in the entire world.

Drawing her knees up to her chin, she wrapped her arms around her legs and let out a contented sigh – a sound that was promptly echoed by a very hot, snuffling breath in her left ear.

'Oi you!' she chuckled, turning away from the sea only to find herself staring directly into Stanley's melting brown eyes.

Stanley sighed, wiggling his expressive eyebrows, and started to pant. Kate grinned and threw an arm around her best friend as the massive bear of a Bernese

Mountain Dog leant his whole weight against her and rested his chin on her shoulder.

Kate planted a kiss on Stanley's nose. 'We'll go in just a sec, I promise,' she said, hugging him.

Kate knew that Stanley would be looking forward to getting back to her tiny little café, The Sardine. Not that he disliked coming on her sandwich rounds with her. In fact, he loved nothing better than riding around in the trailer she hitched to the back of Trixie, her delivery tricycle. Of course, there was always the added bonus that he got fussed to within an inch of his life at every stop they made. But this morning, Kate had left Ethel in charge back at The Sardine, and Stanley wasn't stupid – he knew that his old friend kept a stash of his favourite treats in her apron pocket at all times.

'Home looks so beautiful from here, don't you think?' said Kate, her eyes travelling back inland towards Seabury. From out here on the point where the lighthouse stood, she could almost see the entirety of the little coastal town as it hugged the shoreline and nestled into the arms of the cove.

West Beach was gleaming in the morning sun. Today it was covered with golden sand, but it changed with the tides - sometimes rocky, sometimes sandy - the state of the beach was a daily source of conversation for the locals.

If Kate squinted, she could just about make out The Sardine's striped awning right on the tiny seafront road that overlooked the sandy shore. She wondered if there were customers there right now, enjoying a morning coffee at the little tables she'd set up outside before she'd set off. She knew she was biased, but there wasn't a better place in the whole world to enjoy your morning coffee than sitting outside The Sardine, staring out across West Beach.

Seabury had two beaches that were separated by The Kings Nose - a grassy, rocky outcrop that stuck out into the sea. By some weird geographical hiccup, North Beach was actually west of West Beach and was covered by large, smooth grey pebbles. No one could figure out quite how this was the case because there was no sign of any similar rock for miles around.

The locals just took the weird naming anomaly in their stride, but visitors found it amusing and confusing in equal measures. Several years ago, one incomer had launched a campaign to change the names of the beaches to something more "factually accurate". The campaign didn't last very long. Funnily enough, neither did the newbie.

They didn't really get many visitors in Seabury - something most of the locals were quite happy about. The single coast road that passed through the town was narrow and winding, and Seabury wasn't sign-posted from the main road at all. This tended to keep out the majority of tourists, who found their way to the larger resort towns further along the coast instead.

Of course, there was always talk about *improvements.* Making Seabury *better.* Plans to bring in more visitors. More business. A few people wanted the town opened up... developed. Kate shuddered. Change of any kind wasn't something she was very good at dealing with. She loved the place just as it was - just as it had always been. Thankfully, most of the locals were of the same mind. It seemed to be an ongoing battle - but it was one worth fighting.

Luckily, a recent plan to develop the surrounding area and widen the access road had been put paid to by the discovery of some particularly rare wildlife - endangered moths or something like that. Kate wasn't really sure if they were real or not - she'd yet to meet anyone who'd actually *seen* one of these mythical beasts. Still, fictitious or not, they'd been the perfect excuse to kick the developer's plans into the long grass. Now all she had to put up with was the strange dietary requirements of the visiting ecologists who turned up to study the moths - but that was a small price to pay to keep Seabury just the way it should be.

Kate took another deep lung-full of sea air and closed her eyes for a moment, listening to the gulls as they swooped overhead. She'd lived in Seabury all her life. Well – *almost* all her life. There had been that three-month blip where she'd moved to London to be with Tom – but the less time she spent thinking about him the better! They'd been together for less than a year, but he'd now managed to be a thorn in her side for *way* longer than that.

London *definitely* hadn't been for her – neither had

marriage, come to that. Three months in and Kate had given it up for a bad job and returned to Seabury – the only place that she ever wanted to call home again. She'd dropped straight back into her life here, took the boarding down from the café windows, fired up her cranky old Italian coffee machine, and did her best to pretend that the interruption had never happened.

Whatever. Today was shaping up to be a perfectly lovely day and she wasn't going to ruin it by thinking about all that crap... and Tom... and everything she'd almost given up for him. Nope. Nuh-uh.

She couldn't believe she'd even considered leaving everything she had here. If Seabury was home then the locals were her family - the only family she had left these days other than Stanley. She hadn't been back long before he'd appeared in her life, looking for love and a new home. Suddenly she had the best friend a girl could ever ask for. A best friend that, right now, was nudging her in the ribs with his nose.

'All right. Let's get back to work,' she chuckled, hauling herself to her feet. Stanley followed suit, wafting his feathery tail back and forth, ready to follow her wherever she went next.

Kate turned and laid a palm against the stone wall of the old lighthouse for a brief moment. 'See you soon,' she whispered.

The lighthouse was derelict having been decommissioned years ago. As far as she knew, no one else ever bothered to come out here, but in Kate's eyes, it was the most beautiful, magical place in the entire world. It held some of her most precious memories. Her dad used to bring her up here to play when she was little, and she'd spent many an hour as a teenager with her back propped against the wall, a book abandoned in her lap as she stared out to sea.

It belonged to the town council now, and Kate lived with a kind of constant, low-lying dread that they'd do something ridiculous like tear it down or sell it to some developer. But, for now, it sat here on the point - mostly forgotten - standing sentry over Seabury.

Kate jumped as a wet nose nudged at her free hand, and she looked down at Stanley, who was staring at her with his eyebrows raised. He really did have the best eyebrows in the world - and they tended to go into overdrive when he was hungry.

'Okay boy, you're right,' she laughed. 'We'd better go and make sure Ethel hasn't been overrun - race you!'

She patted her thigh then hurtled back over towards Trixie. Turning to look for Stanley, she let out a laugh. He was ambling towards her, taking his own sweet time. Before he'd come to live with her, Stanley had been the companion of an elderly gent, and he still moved at a pace to suit a frail eighty-something-year-old, even though the vet had assured her that he was still a relatively young dog, and in perfect health.

There wasn't any need for Kate to coax Stanley up into the trailer though – he hopped up and settled in happily, just as he had done on the first day he'd joined her on her delivery round.

Kate had bought Trixie's trailer to carry extra stock and to make it easier for her to collect produce from the allotments - not as a taxi for a great big hairy passenger - but she didn't mind in the slightest. There was plenty of room for her orders as well as Stanley's pillow. Besides, there would be an outcry from her customers if she didn't bring him with her.

Stanley was universally adored, and that was just the way he liked it. He'd become the unofficial therapy dog for the entire town - welcomed into farms and offices alike - and greeted with just as much enthusiasm as Kate's delicious deliveries - if not more!

They'd finished their rounds for today and as usual, Stanley had been well and truly loved on. Now it was time to take Trixie back to her little yard next to The Sardine and then let Ethel off the hook. Kate couldn't be more grateful to her old friend for stepping in and covering the café - but she *was* somewhere in her seventies (Kate would never dream of asking her exact age!) and she didn't want to leave her on her own for too long.

'All right lad, here we go,' she called over her shoulder as she hopped up onto the saddle and pedalled out onto the narrow road that wound downhill all the way back into the centre of Seabury.

This was the bit of the trip Kate liked best – with her deliveries done, the hard pedalling work was complete, and she could now freewheel back down towards the sea.

She let out a great whoop of delight as they sped past a couple of the outlying cottages, Trixie just a pink and red blur reflected in the windows as they pelted past. There was an echoing woof from Stanley in the back and Kate giggled.

She hadn't realised how much she'd needed a little break this morning - just a few minutes out of her busy day to remind herself that she was exactly where she wanted to be, doing exactly what she wanted to do, surrounded by the people she loved.

As much as she tried to push it to the back of her mind, this whole divorce malarkey had been a bit tough to take at times. Kate hated change. She hated confrontation. She hated fuss. Unfortunately, getting a divorce from a complete nincompoop came with a massive dollop of all three. Still – it was all pretty much done and dusted now. Almost. Kinda.

Anyway - thank heavens for Ethel. She'd spotted Kate heading for a mini meltdown when the post had arrived that morning bearing yet another manilla envelope from Tom's solicitor. Her old friend had whipped it out of her hands, ushered her out of the café to do her rounds, and insisted that Kate should take a breather before she came back. When Kate had tried to make a grab for the envelope, Ethel had just folded it in half and stuffed it into the pocket of her voluminous apron.

'You know there's nothing in there that can't wait,' she'd stated, making Kate laugh despite herself. Of course, as usual, Ethel was right - whatever Tom wanted, it could wait until *she* was ready for a change.

Kate slowed to pedal at a more sedate speed through the heart of Seabury, passing North Beach with the Post Office, *Nana's* Ice Cream parlour, and the cavernous, empty surf shop with its *For Sale* sign. It was such a shame that the place was still empty - but there was a ridiculous price on it, and who needed such a vast space in the middle of a sleepy town?

'Morning Stanley!' cried an upright gent as they trundled past The Pebble Street Hotel that stood on the boundary of The King's Nose. 'Morning Kate!'

'Hi Lionel! Painting today?' she called back.

Lionel nodded. 'Yep – as soon as I've had my morning exercise, followed by my Sardine fix!' he grinned. 'You *are* open today, I assume?'

'Of course!' Kate nodded. 'Ethel's been manning the fort, but I'm heading back now.'

'Thank heavens for that. Veronica's got us on even shorter rations than usual this week!'

'See you in a bit then!' said Kate as she pulled away from him.

Lionel touched his hand to his straw hat and then waved goodbye to Stanley.

Kate tutted and shook her head. Veronica Hughes was a piece of work. To say that she wasn't very generous would be putting it mildly - she was about as mean spirited as a person could get. Kate prided herself on her ability to see the best in people, but even *she* struggled when it came to Veronica.

Lionel Barclay, however, was a sweetheart. He lived in a suite on the very top floor of The Pebble Street Hotel. He'd been there for what felt like forever - certainly since before Veronica had purchased the place.

The old hotel was a beautiful building that, in its heyday, had welcomed visitors who were looking for a spot of luxury. Veronica now ran it as a budget bed and breakfast - not that the "budget" part was reflected in her prices.

It was Veronica's dearest wish to chuck Lionel out, but he wasn't going anywhere. He had the only copy of the key to his rooms, and Veronica wasn't even allowed through the door. Lionel being allowed to remain in his suite for as long as he wanted to had been one of the conditions of the sale of the hotel – a condition that he was going to make Veronica stick to, no matter how much she hated it.

Kate grinned to herself. She was pretty sure Lionel rather liked being the thorn in Veronica's side. He paid his rent and kept himself to himself. The fact that his rooms boasted the best views in the entire place was Veronica's tough luck.

Lionel himself was a bit of an enigma. He was a retired something or other – no one was quite sure what... admiral? Banker? Historian? There were plenty of stories floating around, but none of them had been confirmed.

Always impeccably dressed, he had been one of her earliest regulars when she'd first opened The Sardine. He'd been heartbroken when she'd shut up shop to move to London and was the first back when she'd reopened. She still swore that he'd had a tear in his eye that day, but Lionel was having none of it.

'Right, Stanley lad,' said Kate, as they rounded the curve in the road that brought them in sight of West Beach and The Sardine, 'here we are, nearly home.'

Kate held out her hand to indicate that she was pulling Trixie into the yard - and then promptly applied the brakes, dropped her arm and swore loudly. Stanley let out a low bark of disgust in agreement.

'I know!' muttered Kate. 'Inconsiderate a-holes!'

There, parked right across the entrance to Trixie's yard, was a massive, expensive-looking estate car.

CHAPTER 2

'Wow - my plan didn't work then?' said Ethel, her eyebrows raised as Kate stormed into The Sardine.

'Huh?' she muttered distractedly, watching as Stanley rounded the counter to sit on Ethel's toes, leaning his head against her as he stared up at her adoringly.

'Hello, you beautiful boy, at least you're in a good mood!' chuckled Ethel, rummaging in her apron pocket for one of Stanley's biscuits - which disappeared with much eyebrow wiggling. 'So - what happened?' she demanded, turning her attention back to Kate.

'Oh nothing,' Kate sighed, heading to the sink to wash her hands. 'Just some plonker's gone and parked right across the yard again so I can't put Trixie away.'

'Ah!' said Ethel nodding. 'That explains the face then.'

'Face?' said Kate, drying her hands on a checked tea towel, then lifting the lid on one of the cake stands and half-inching a piece of her favourite Victoria sponge.

'Yes - your face!' exclaimed Ethel. 'You're lucky there aren't any customers in here - you'd have terrified them with that face!'

Kate shook her head and sighed. 'Sorry.'

Ethel shrugged. 'No need to apologise to me, it's your café! Just like that's your own stock you're stealing,' she smirked as Kate stuffed half the slice of cream and jam-filled heaven into her gob.

Kate rolled her eyes in delight as the sponge melted in her mouth. She let out a groan. Ethel made all the cakes for The Sardine and there was no getting away from it - they were the best in the county. In fact, they were so good that Ethel had been banned from entering any of the local shows because it "just wasn't fair to the other entrants." Ethel didn't seem to mind too much - in fact, she wore it as a badge of honour.

Kate swallowed, the rush of sugar knocking the edge off her anger. 'It's just so bloody inconsiderate though,' she said, taking another bite.

'I know, love.'

'I mean - there's a sign and everything. Can't these people read?!'

'Maybe not...' said Ethel, feeding Stanley another

biscuit, 'but I expect it's just a visitor who doesn't realise how things work around here, that's all.'

'Bloomin' visitors,' muttered Kate.

'Now don't be like that,' said Ethel, taking a cloth and going over to wipe the already clean tables. 'You know you need them to survive.'

Kate shook her head. 'I'm here for the locals.'

'Yes, I know. But it's good for everyone if there's a little bit more money coming into the town. Locals have to have something to live on other than the beauty of Seabury, you know.'

Kate nodded. 'I know.'

'Otherwise, we'll end up with more empty shops like the surf shop - and nowhere for the youngsters to work.'

Kate nodded again. 'I know.' She loved Ethel dearly, having known her all her life - but her old friend could make her feel like a naughty schoolgirl when she was in one of her moods.

'Actually,' said Kate, finishing up the cake and doing her best not to eyeball a second slice, 'that's reminded me - I need to get on and advertise for a replacement for Claire.'

Ethel nodded. 'No rush. You know I'll help out as long as you need me to.'

Kate smiled at her gratefully. Claire had been with her for what felt like forever. She'd been her only member of staff other than when Ethel popped in to help out during the busy summer months. But Claire had left Seabury three weeks ago to live with her boyfriend in one of the larger towns just along the coast. The problem was, Claire had always just... fitted in. Kate dreaded trying to find the perfect replacement. She wasn't even sure if such a thing existed.

That was the thing with The Sardine – just as the name suggested, it was tiny. Small but perfectly formed or, as one of the locals had dubbed it, *The Smallest Café in the World.*

There was just about enough space inside for a couple of chairs and tables, the counter and the kitchen. The open plan meant that everything was piled in together. The effect was cosy and eclectic.

In the summer, the tables outside on the pavement under the awning doubled Kate's seating space, but in the winter, when she stashed the awning indoors to stop the wind ripping it to pieces, everyone piled inside, and things got even more intimate. Right next to her oven there was an old, wood-fired stove that was incredibly handy when there was a power cut - which happened fairly regularly.

A bit like with a ship's galley, everything in The Sardine had its place - it was the only way to make such a small space work. That's why it was important to have the right people working there. Or – the right person, she should say. It was, after all, Kate's home as well as her workplace. She lived on the two levels above the café, and it took a lot for her to trust people to treat The Sardine with as much love as she did.

Luckily, for now, she had Ethel.

'Thanks so much for this morning by the way,' said Kate gratefully, smiling at her friend and making an effort to shrug off the funk that had landed on her.

'You know it's my pleasure, Kate!' said Ethel. 'It was quite a busy morning actually - not that it looks like it now.'

'Not too much for you, I hope?' she said.

'Of course not - just the usual suspects wanting their toasted teacakes and gallons of coffee!'

'Speaking of usual suspects, I saw Lionel - he's on his way over,' said Kate, turning to her cantankerous old coffee machine - dubbed the Italian Stallion by Claire. There were very few people who could get a decent cup of java out of it. You had to talk to the machine nicely - that was the key.

Kate loaded up the puck and inhaled. Hm - maybe that's what she needed to set her back on course for the day - a good hit of rich, aromatic coffee.

'Bless Lionel,' said Ethel, replenishing the pile of teacakes under the glass dome on the counter, 'he's probably coming in for a top-up on his breakfast - I reckon Veronica's new plan is to starve him out of the hotel.'

Kate shook her head. 'Not on my watch!'

'Indeed. Well, you've still got a good few pots of my marmalade left, so he'll be alright.'

Veronica was notoriously mean, and Kate had heard plenty of horror stories from Lionel over the years - old eggs, single rashers of watery bacon, and cereal that was measured out using an eggcup.

Lionel always had the same thing when he came to The Sardine – a strong, milky coffee and two slices of well-done toast spread thinly with homemade marmalade. He preferred Ethel's if he could get it, but as long as Kate never tried to fob him off with any of the "supermarket gloop" Veronica gave her guests, he was happy.

'Actually,' said Ethel, you mentioning Veronica's just reminded me - I ran into her on my walk last night.'

Kate turned and handed her a latte, just the way she liked it.

'Thanks lovely,' she said, taking it over to one of the tables and perching on a chair. 'Yes - you'll never guess what she told me.'

Kate shrugged. Knowing Veronica, it wouldn't be anything nice - though, owing to her propensity for sticking her nose into all kinds of business, she did tend to be a pretty accurate source for all kinds of juicy gossip.

'Apparently, the old surf shop has sold at last.'

'You're joking?!' said Kate, leaning against the counter and raising her eyebrows. 'I was thinking about that when we went past just now. Do we know anything about who's taken it on?' she asked with interest.

She couldn't deny that having such a big, vacant space filled at long last would be good for Seabury - if only so that the pretty stretch overlooking North Beach wasn't marred by the gaping hole that was the boarded-up shop.

'Well...' said Ethel, 'I'm not sure you're going to like this.'

Kate's attention was instantly caught by the concern on her old friend's face.

'Why? How bad's it going to be?' she said with a laugh. 'Unless of course, you're about to tell me Tom's decided to move to Seabury just to make my life a living hell?'

Ethel went to say something and then paused, looking anxious.

'Okay - now you're scaring me!' said Kate. 'He's not, is he?'

'Tom?' said Ethel. 'No of course not.'

'Well then?!' said Kate, starting to get impatient.

'Well... Veronica told me it's going to be another café. One of those big, posh New York Froth affairs,' said Ethel, not taking her eyes off Kate - clearly waiting for her reaction. 'Of course, you know Veronica - she could just be stirring!'

'Oh - she's definitely stirring,' sighed Kate, 'but yes, I do know Veronica - so do you - and you *know* her gossip tends to be spot on. She's probably got it directly from the estate agents or the council.'

Ethel nodded. 'Sounds like Veronica.'

'Well...' said Kate, blowing out a breath. 'It's not the best news I've had today - but I'm not worried.'

'You're not?' asked Ethel, raising her eyebrows.

'Nope,' said Kate with a determined smile and a shake of the head. 'I've been here a long time. I've got my regulars and my sandwich round on Trixie. I know everyone and everyone knows me. I'm sure there's more than enough business to go around... these new guys will just have to cater to all these visitors people keep trying to bring into Seabury.'

Ethel grinned at her. 'Good for you, love!' she said, pride shining in her eyes. 'There's the girl your dad was proud of.'

The words brought an instant lump to Kate's throat, but she beamed with pride nonetheless. Her dad had been gone several years now - but it was amazing how much she still missed him.

'Thanks Ethel.'

'Hello ladies!' The cheery call came from the doorway, and they both swung around to greet Lionel as he strode in, rosy-cheeked from his walk in the sunshine.

'Hello deary! Your usual?' asked Ethel, getting to her feet and indicating for Lionel to take the table.

'Of course. Nothing better. Hello again, Stanley old boy!' he said, reaching down to ruffle the big bear's ears as he wandered over to greet the newcomer. 'Now then, how would you like a bit of toast when it arrives?'

'Don't go spoiling my dog,' laughed Kate as she got busy and fired up the Italian Stallion again.

'Why ever not? He loves it!' chuckled Lionel.

'Because my poor little legs won't be able to pedal

Trixie up that hill if he puts on any more puppy-fat!' she laughed.

In all fairness to Stanley, he was exactly the same size he'd always been - huge - and she wouldn't have him any other way. But it *was* a miracle that he didn't explode, given the number of titbits he was slipped each day in the café by his adoring fans.

Kate delivered Lionel's coffee and set the table for him while Ethel piled up his toast and brought it over with a dish of marmalade.

'Thank you!' he sighed, grabbing a knife and slathering a good dollop of the golden preserve onto his toast. He took a massive bite and sighed with bliss. 'Heaven,' he said as soon as he'd swallowed his mouthful. 'Ethel, you really are a wonder!'

'Oh, get on with you!' she laughed.

'I'm serious, it's no wonder Charlie's smitten.'

Kate watched with interest as Ethel turned a rather fetching shade of pink and bustled back to the kitchen without saying a word.

'Something I said?' asked Lionel under his breath, quirking an eyebrow at Kate.

'Erm... yes, I think so!' she replied quietly.

Everyone knew that old Charlie Endicott was head over heels in love with Ethel. Charlie was Lionel's best friend, and they made a rather unlikely pair - the dapper artist and the salt-of-the-earth gardener.

Charlie spent most of his waking life at the allotments, tending to his prize-winning veg. In fact, he grew most of the veggies for The Sardine. Kate loved nothing better than when a customer dared to ask about "food miles". She'd lead them outside and point to the hill on the far side of Seabury where the allotments lay, with their patchwork of plots, dotted with colourful little sheds.

Charlie was a good, kind soul - but rather lacking in the words department. He was someone who tended to show you how he felt, rather than tell you. Somehow, though, she doubted the regular batches of luscious strawberries, raspberries, rhubarb and gooseberries he sent to Ethel had *quite* managed to convey the extent of his true feelings.

Kate was pretty certain that Ethel knew Charlie felt *something* for her - after all, most of the locals had ribbed her about it at some point. But she'd never once seen her friend react with anything other than a cheerful "get away with you" when anyone mentioned it. This rather more teenaged reaction was new. Kate made a mental note to ask her what was going on when they were in private.

'So,' said Lionel. 'Have you heard the old surf shop's being turned into a café?'

His clumsy attempt at a change of subject made him wince as it quickly dawned on him that he'd jumped from the frying pan into the fire when it came to controversial topics of conversation. Kate decided to let the poor guy off the hook.

'Yep - great news that there'll be something in there

after all this time, isn't it?' she said cheerfully.

'I like your attitude, young lady,' said Lionel warmly, taking another bite of his toast.

Kate just smiled at him and decided to grab the lull in conversation caused by much chewing as an excuse to quickly duck outside for a moment. She was just about the head through the door when a man barged into the café and she bumped straight into him.

'Ooff!' grunted Kate as she bounced off his front, the surprise of the collision knocking the breath out of her. She steadied herself and straightened up, only to find the man brushing down the front of his very expensive-looking suit.

'I'm so sorry,' she said, forcing a polite smile onto her face. 'I didn't see you coming.'

'Clearly,' he harrumphed.

Kate felt her spine stiffen and she stared at him. He wasn't a local. She'd definitely remember if she'd seen his face around before. Sharp cheekbones. Cold grey eyes peering out from under a dark, swept-back mop of hair. Stern. Stroppy. Maybe he'd be quite attractive if he smiled, but it didn't look like that was something he did very often. Or- *at all*. She thought he was probably in his late thirties - or maybe a little bit older. It was hard to tell with all the glowering he was doing.

'Can I get you a coffee?' she asked. 'On the house, of course!' she added. After all, she *had* just managed to body-check him on his way in.

'No. But you can tell me who the *hell* owns that

monstrosity that's blocking me in?!' he demanded, glaring at the three of them in turn.

Kate felt something shift behind her, and the next thing she knew Stanley had ambled over from crumb-duty under Lionel's table and plonked himself down between her and the guy. He didn't growl - but he did fix his eyes on the man's face, his tail unusually still.

'Get away from me,' muttered the man, taking a step back.

Kate raised her eyebrows in surprise. Stanley was the least threatening dog she'd ever met. He was basically an oversized teddy bear who loved nothing more than a good cuddle, but this stranger was staring at him like he was some kind of crazed attack-dog.

'He's friendly,' said Kate, gently laying her hand on Stanley's huge head, fighting down the urge to add *"unlike you".*

'He shouldn't be in a public place.'

Kate bristled. She'd already had enough of this idiot. Messing with her was one thing, but *no one* messed with her dog.

'He's not in a *public place* - he's in my café. His home. If you've got a problem with that, you're more than welcome to leave.'

'Trust me - there's nothing that would give me more pleasure - but you've blocked me in with your... your... pile of scrap metal.'

Kate fought the urge to growl at him herself. 'I parked Trixie next to your car because you've blocked the access to my yard - where she belongs,' she said. She didn't like her voice like this - all hard and angry. The sooner she got rid of this git, the better.

'Trixie?!' he said incredulously. 'You've given that pile of rust a name?'

Kate's hands bunched into fists, and she fought the urge to push this idiot backwards and physically remove him from the café.

'Just don't park there again.'

'It's not double-yellowed.'

'There's a sign.'

'It's hand-painted - hardly legal!'

'You're blocking access to my private property. You're lucky I didn't have you towed!' growled Kate, causing Stanley to stand up.

The guy's reaction was instant. He backed up a couple more paces looking petrified.

Good. The further away he was from her, the less likely it was that she'd "accidentally" punch him on the nose for being a prick.

'Okay, okay. Just get out of my way and I'll move the car,' he muttered.

'Honestly,' said Kate. 'Tourists!'

'*Excuse* me!' he said. 'I'm not a tourist. I live here.'

'Rubbish,' said Kate firmly.

'These say otherwise,' he said, taking a bunch of keys out of his pocket and rattling them at her.

'Goodness.' Ethel's voice behind her made Kate

jump. She'd forgotten for a moment there was anyone else here.

'Huh. Great. Well,' said Kate, feeling wrong-footed. 'Welcome to Seabury,' she huffed.

'Thanks!' the guy smirked. 'I'm Mike Pendle by the way. I own New York Froth.'

CHAPTER 3

Kate was still fuming by the time she'd finished tucking Trixie up in the yard. She paused for a moment and patted the handlebars, trying to suck up some of the joy the tricycle's bright pink paint job and jaunty red handlebars usually brought her... but right now, it just wasn't working.

Trixie lived out here in the yard all year round. Sure, Kate threw an old tarp over her when the weather was bad - well weighted down to stop the mad, swirling gusts of wind off the sea from stealing it away. But still, the salty air meant that every year, Kate cleaned Trixie down and gave her a new paint job. She was particularly fond of this year's colour combo - though she had to admit, the six-year-old inside her still missed the orange and green polka dots from the previous year.

Anyway - no matter what that... that... *blow-in* said, Trixie was definitely not a "pile of scrap metal!"

'Don't listen to that git,' Kate whispered, patting Trixie again. *'I* love you.'

'First sign of madness you know!'

Kate whirled around to find her friend Paula peering at her with a grin on her face.

'First sign? You know I'm way past that!' laughed Kate, opening her arms and pulling her friend into a hug. 'Swimming today?' she asked, linking arms with Paula and heading back out of the yard.

Paula shook her head. 'Nah - tomorrow. We're back to our usual Wednesday morning. We only shifted last week around because I had that appointment. Anyway - that's why I was popping in - wondered if we could change in The Sardine again?'

'Of course!' said Kate. 'You know you never need to ask!'

Paula was a founding member and trouble-maker-in-chief of the Chilly Dippers, Seabury's wild swimming club. She often joked that it sounded a lot more daring than it actually was. Skinny dipping was frowned upon, but not entirely outlawed, and their members were mostly made up of a group of what might be described as "older and wiser" local women. It wasn't that men were excluded... it was just the way things had worked out.

The group boasted a wide variety of splashing and swimming styles and you only had to go in as far as your ankles to be considered a proper "Dipper" - and that was just about a far as many of them ever went. Kate, however, was full of admiration for them. They were a tight-knit group, and they went in the sea come rain or shine - all year around.

Sometimes Stanley liked to join them for a swim, and the group always loved having him. Kate had cottoned on pretty quickly to the fact that it was a good idea to attach a float to him so that they could keep an eye on his whereabouts. No matter how much he hated having a bath, Stanley loved to swim - and liked nothing better than heading straight out to sea in search of some friendly seals to play with. Kate had had to get someone to go out in a boat to collect him from these impromptu playdates more than once.

When the weather was particularly bad, with the rain lashing horizontally across the beach, Kate would open the café early so that the Chilly Dippers could come in to change in the dry. Wednesday mornings were always a rowdy time in the café because the Dippers would invariably pile in after their swim, steaming up the windows and warming up with bowls of Kate's hearty, homemade soup that she made specially for them in the winter, or with hot drinks, pastries and plenty of cake in the summer.

'Coming in for a coffee, then?' Kate asked, glancing at Paula and noticing, not for the first time over the past few weeks, that her friend looked pale and rather tired.

Paula nodded. 'Yes please. And the biggest piece of cake you can find... if you haven't eaten all of it yet?'

'I *might* have left you a slice,' laughed Kate.

'Perfect. Then you can tell me why you were declaring your undying love to your tricycle and muttering about a "git".

Kate snorted. 'Okay, deal. And you can tell me how your appointment went last week,' she said, holding the café door open for her friend.

Paula shot her a look and shrugged. 'Nothing to tell. A few blood tests, no biggie!' she said lightly. 'Morning Ethel, hi ya Lionel!' she said cheerily, striding over to the counter to investigate the cake stands.

Kate watched her closely. She knew Paula's answer should put her mind at ease, but she couldn't help the nagging sensation that her friend wasn't telling her everything. Ah well, all in good time.

'Rhubarb streusel cake!' Paula sighed in delight. 'Ethel, you're a marvel!'

Ethel smiled and cut her a mammoth slice.

'Made with Charlie's prize rhubarb too,' added Kate, watching Ethel's face closely. There it was again - that fetching pink blush spreading across the older woman's cheeks. Curiouser and curiouser!

'Right Kate lovely - I'd better go,' said Ethel, bustling around behind the counter and keeping her back to them while she grabbed her handbag and bits and bobs.

'Of course!' said Kate, glancing at her watch. 'Sugar, I'm so sorry - I hadn't realised it was that time already!'

'It's no problem dear. That man's got you all of a dither!' said Ethel, going over to give Stanley a final pat and another sneaky bit of biscuit, which he wolfed down.

'Man?' demanded Paula. 'Kate Hardy, you've been withholding important information. Is it that French bloke? Has he finally decided to settle down a bit?'

'Chance would be a fine thing,' muttered Ethel.

'You two!' said Kate. 'No - it has absolutely nothing to do with Pierre. And just for your information, I don't want him to "settle down", I like things exactly how they are, thank you very much.'

'But you never know when you're going to see him next,' said Paula indignantly. 'He just... shows up!'

'He does text sometimes,' she laughed, 'and anyway, what's so wrong with that? A little bit of spontaneous romance never hurt anyone!'

'Neither does a bit of commitment,' said Ethel.

'Tried that, didn't like it,' grumbled Kate as the image of Tom flashed in front of her eyes.

'Only because you tried it with an idiot,' said Paula.

'Exactly,' agreed Ethel.

'Rubbish,' said Kate. 'Anyway - I a*m* committed - to this place, and Stanley, and Seabury, and my friends...'

'None of which are going to keep you warm at night!' said Paula, raising her eyebrows.

Kate was about to argue that actually, having

Stanley weighing down the duvet was like sleeping next to a furnace some nights, but she thought better of it.

'Paula's right, Kate. I know you're practically married to this place and to Seabury, but don't let it get in the way of you finding true love. It's a rare thing, and when it happens...'

Kate frowned as an unusually sober look passed across Ethel's face. 'Okay,' she said, forcing a laugh and trying to lighten the mood. 'If Pierre tries to whisk me away to France with him, I'll give it some serious thought!'

'You're hopeless!' said Ethel, kissing her on the cheek and heading for the door. 'See you tomorrow?'

'I'll be here if I'm not already in France!'

Ethel snorted and disappeared through the door.

'So - if it wasn't your French shag-buddy you were muttering about just now, who was it?' asked Paula, sipping her coffee and watching as Kate busied herself in the kitchen.

'Urgh - just this absolute knob head who blocked the yard this morning so I couldn't get Trixie back in there.'

'Nothing unusual about that,' chuckled Paula. It happened at least once a week during the summer months - hence Kate's decision to put up some signs.

'No - but most of them are apologetic when they realise what they've done. This guy burst in here, was rude about Trixie and then announced that he's the new owner of the old surf shop.'

'Mike Pendle?'

'You *know* him?!' demanded Kate.

'Nope - but I know *of* him. He built New York Froth up from scratch - had a whole bunch of them along the coast. You must have heard his name before - I mean, he was in all the magazines - won all the business awards as South West's very own fancy-pants coffee chain.'

'Eewww gross!' whined Kate. 'How on *earth* did he get permission to come to Seabury?! I mean - that's not what the town needs, is it?! A horrible chain moving in?!'

'Not a chain anymore,' said Paula, draining the dregs from her cup and leaning back in her chair. 'Apparently, his wife got everything in the divorce... all apart from the company name! So he's got to start from scratch again - without his flagship café.'

'Oh no, my heart breaks for him,' Kate deadpanned, bending to pop a couple of savoury pies in the oven.

'I thought you'd be a bit more sympathetic!' said Paula, clearly surprised that her usually kind and caring friend was being so uncharacteristically cold. 'I mean - imagine if Tom had taken this place from you in the divorce.'

Kate straightened up, a horrible swooping sensation going through her.

'Yeah... well...' she said, suddenly realising that she

still hadn't opened the manilla envelope from Tom's solicitor. It was probably still tucked away in Ethel's discarded apron. 'You didn't see how obnoxious this *Mike Pendle* was earlier.'

'He *is* quite handsome though, don't you think?' said Paula with a sly grin. 'I've seen his picture. Dark hair, kind of dashing in a brooding way...'

Kate shook her head. 'A person who is that stroppy is *not* handsome. He looked like he spent most of his time chewing wasps. And he called Trixie a monstrosity, *plus* he didn't look like he knew how to smile if his life depended on it.'

'Methinks you protesteth too much,' laughed Paula.

Kate shook her head decidedly. 'Nope - if anything I protesteth too little. I mean - he didn't like Stanley!' she said as if this was the end of the matter.

'How could anyone not like Stanley?' said Paula, looking surprised, and glancing with affection at the massive black, white and tan mound of fur snoozing in the corner.

'Exactly,' said Kate.

'So...'

'What?'

'What are you going to do?' she said, a note of worry creeping into her voice. 'I mean, about New York Froth coming to town?'

'Absolutely nothing,' said Kate with a big smile that was decidedly braver than she was feeling. 'Sounds like the deal is done, so there's no point in me whining about it, is there? Besides, the old surf shop's in a state - it'll take him a good few months to get ready to open. I'll just keep doing what I'm doing, make the most of the summer, look after my customers, deliver my sandwiches and keep serving the best coffee in Seabury.'

'And when he *does* open up?'

'Well... I'm sure there are plenty of coffee addicts in this town for the both of us. And besides, a little bit of friendly competition never hurt anyone!'

CHAPTER 4

It was one of those days when Kate thanked her lucky stars that her commute was so short. She'd kept a warm smile plastered on her face all day, greeting customers, making toasties and serving coffees, bantering, laughing and reassuring every single one of them that *no she wasn't at all worried about New York Froth opening* and *yes, it would be brilliant for the town.*

She'd managed to keep a lid on the low-level anxiety that had been bubbling away in her gut ever since she'd got back from her delivery round. But now, as she walked the ten paces from The Sardine's door to her flat door just around the corner, she couldn't wait to be safely back in her own space. She needed the freedom to examine how she was feeling, without the fear of those feelings showing on her face.

'Here you go Stanley boy,' she murmured, pushing the door open for him. Just as he did every day, Stanley ambled up the steep wooden stairs in front of her, heading up to her flat that sat snugly above the café.

In her head, Kate still called it a flat, but in reality, it was a maisonette - narrow and tall - with a cosy living room and galley kitchen on the first floor and her bathroom and bedroom at the top.

By the time she'd reached the first floor, Kate peered into the living room to find Stanley already sitting in his giant bed in front of the wood burner - just as she'd expected. The fire wasn't lit - but that never put him off. This had been Stanley's routine ever since he'd come to live with her - at the end of a busy day in the café, he'd retreat to his bed for a nap - bonus points if the fire was lit!

Kate knelt down next to him and stroked his silky ears for a moment, trying to let the calm of her sanctuary wash over her. She took in a deep breath and let it out as a laugh when Stanley matched her sigh and flopped sideways, tongue lolling.

'I know what you mean!' she said, gazing at him adoringly. This was why Stanley was her best friend - no matter how she was feeling, he always made her day better just by being himself.

Stanley wasn't *really* her dog, although these days, he was never far from her side. He'd come into her life not long after she'd returned to Seabury from her ill-fated attempt at London life.

He'd originally belonged to an old man called Harold, who'd lived in one of the cottages on the outskirts of Seabury. Shortly after Harold had passed away, his family descended on the cottage, emptied the place of all his belongings and put it on the market - all within a week. Of course, it had promptly been snapped up as a holiday home.

Their work done and the money pocketed, the family left Seabury just as suddenly as they'd arrived - leaving Stanley behind to fend for himself.

People had reported seeing him wandering around the town, but it had taken a while for them all to realise what had happened. Then, on a particularly wet, blustery evening, Kate had opened her door to find him sitting there, looking sad but hopeful. She'd let him in - of course she had - and Stanley had made his way slowly up the stairs, found a place for himself in front of the wood burner, and curled up to sleep.

It still made Kate's heart squeeze when she thought of how sad and lonely he must have been after losing his owner like that - only to be turfed out of his house and abandoned. *How* anyone could be so cruel as to just leave him behind was beyond her. She bent low and kissed his soft, snoozing head.

'Right boy, I'll be back in a bit, okay?' she whispered.

Stanley didn't even open an eye, which made Kate crack a genuine smile. He wouldn't budge for a good hour now that he'd crashed out.

She stood up and stretched, looking around her

living room. It was light and bright and full of shells and driftwood from her wanderings along the beaches. The walls were covered in little paintings by Lionel - scenes from around the town, the Chilly Dippers, the sun rising, the sun setting, the ebb and flow of life in a seaside town. Even here in her home, she surrounded herself with her one true love - Seabury.

But the magic of her little sanctuary wasn't working on her this evening. The knot of unspoken worry was still there, sitting low in her stomach. Well - there was only one cure as far as she knew!

Kate twiddled with the bath tap until the water was gushing at full pelt into the tub. If ever there was a day for a bubble bath that was full to within an inch of the top of the tub, it was today.

As she swished the water with one hand, watching the bubbles mounting into white, fluffy peaks, she reached out and took a sip of wine before placing the glass carefully back on the corner of the bath.

Now then, was she ready to finally take a proper, logical look at what was worrying her? Wine? Check. Bubble bath? Almost ready. Okay. It was time.

She'd been putting a brave face on the New York Froth news all day - assuring locals that it wouldn't be a problem for The Sardine, that nothing would change, and she was *happy* that a new business was opening and filling the sad, empty space that used to be the surf shop - but how much of that did she actually believe? After all - it *was* more change.

She reached for the bottle of lavender oil she kept on the mantlepiece and splashed a few drops into the already bubble-laden water. Why not? She needed all the additional relaxation vibes she could muster.

It wasn't as though she was worried that The Sardine would struggle with this new competition... of course it wouldn't. Would it?

Kate took another deep, steadying breath. She needed to look at the facts. She had a thriving delivery round that was just about as full as she could manage if she was going to continue to deliver on Trixie. It was local - and that was the whole point of it - the way she liked it. She couldn't cycle any further than she already did every day, and she didn't want to start delivering by car.

On top of that, the café was pretty much always busy - she certainly never had any cake left at the end of the day! Plus it was relatively cheap to run because it was so small, the most she needed was one member of staff - plus Ethel.

There was the rub, though - the thing that had been quietly bugging her. Her business was full to capacity. It survived and it supported her - but there was no room to grow. And if she *did* lose any custom because of New York Froth, she might well run into problems.

But she didn't need to worry about that, did she?

Her customers were loyal. Mike Pendle wouldn't be able to open for a good month or two, and besides, he'd be catering to a very different set of customers anyway. She'd keep her locals, and he could deal with the visitors and second home owners. Hell - she'd even throw in the blasted ecologists who came to study the mythical moths if he wanted them - it would save her a fortune on buying the fancy-pants alternative milks they always seemed so keen on.

Yep - she would put New York Froth to the back of her mind and stop worrying about it. Straight away. Yes she would.

Yes she would, yes she would, yes she would.

Balls.

It wasn't working. Her mind was spiralling, and she could feel her logical, sensible side giving in to mounting, irrational fear.

She turned off the tap and stared at the bath. It was time for drastic action. The bath and the wine weren't going to cut it on their own. It was time to pull out the big guns.

Not for the first, Kate sent up a little prayer of thanks that she had a bathroom with a working fireplace. She adored her whole flat, but this was probably her favourite room. In the depths of winter, there was nothing better than sinking into a deep bath - candles lit, wine or hot chocolate on hand - and the fire crackling away in the grate as she stared up at the stars through the skylight overhead.

Unfortunately, right now, it was the middle of the summer and the room was rather warm, but she wasn't going to let that put her off. A fire would be therapeutic and just what she needed to help her relax.

It didn't take her long before she was submerged in bubbles and a merry little fire was crackling in the grate. She'd opened the skylight as wide as it would go to let some much-needed fresh air into the room - just so she didn't roast. She'd also lit about a dozen candles. Now, this was more like it!

Kate let out a long breath, took another sip of her wine and then rested her head back to watch a couple of fluffy clouds scud across the patch of blue sky visible through the skylight. Yep - this was better. At long last, the tight knots that she'd been carrying around in her shoulders all day started to loosen.

She was okay really, wasn't she? The Sardine wasn't in any trouble, and she'd been going long enough that she could face a little bit of friendly competition. Besides, maybe it really *would* be a good thing for the town. She'd been saying it to customers all day just to prove how *fine* she was with everything, but it was probably true. It *had* to be better that there wasn't a great big empty space like that marring their lovely seafront.

As for Paula's take on Mike Pendle being hot... not so much. She'd stick with her original assessment when it came to that. Sure, he had all the pieces of that particular puzzle - the dark hair, chiselled jaw - and there was no denying that he could wear a suit well. But he was just so... so... arsey - *that* was the word. There was no way she'd ever be attracted to someone that grumpy.

That's why she'd fallen for Pierre. Okay - maybe *fallen for* was the wrong way of putting it. She wasn't in love with Pierre. That was something she'd be very careful about avoiding for the foreseeable. She'd thought what she'd found with Tom was love... but it just turned out to be a failed attempt at escaping the well of sadness inside her.

No - she wasn't in love with Pierre - but they had a wonderful time when he did come to town. He was easy-going and fun. Dark-haired, dark-eyed and quick to laugh. He'd rock up bearing a gift of lobsters from his boat, or some other thoughtful parcel he'd brought her from Brittany. He never stayed more than a night or two and then he was off again. But for Kate, that was the joy of it. No matter what Paula and Ethel thought, she loved the romance of his short visits. They gave her exactly what she needed. She was too busy for a full-time relationship. And besides, Stanley would never forgive her - he liked to keep her to himself as much as possible.

Kate picked up her wine again and swirled it around thoughtfully. There was still something nagging at the back of her mind - that *what if* feeling - but then, that was part and parcel of hating change. Because changes came, no matter what she did, and there was nothing she could do about that. She had her man - or *enough* of her man to keep her happy. She had her business - and things were fine just the way they were. All she needed to do now was find someone to replace Claire. What else was there to worry about?

CHAPTER 5

*S*od it!

Kate tumbled out of bed and disentangled herself from her duvet cover for what felt like the hundredth time. She gave up. Sleep was just not going to happen, was it?

She hadn't been up this early in a *very* long time. It was light outside – but the kind of light that made it feel like the sun hadn't had its first cup of coffee yet.

One of the joys of living above the café was the fact that Kate could literally fall out of bed and be at work in under a minute – and because Ethel did most of the baking, there was never much of a rush for her to get started on the day. But it did mean that she'd become fairly lax about actually getting herself out of bed at a sensible hour.

Not this morning though. After spending the night tossing and turning, winding herself up in the duvet so badly that she'd had to get out of the bed in the middle of the night to straighten everything out - Kate was desperate to get outside and shake the uncomfortable, scrunched up feeling out of her limbs. She badly needed to fill her lungs with the salty sea air. Maybe that would help dispel the gnawing, anxious feeling that had haunted her all night.

Even poor old Stanley had given her a disgusted look when she'd kicked him off his spot on the duvet so that she could remake the bed sometime around midnight. He'd ended up decamping back downstairs to his own bed, sick of her constant wriggling.

Kate pulled on a scruffy pair of jeans and a warm jumper. It might be July, but she knew it would be chilly down on the beach this early in the morning. She nipped into the bathroom, splashed her face with some cold water in an attempt to wake herself up, then made her way down to the living room.

'Fancy a walk?'

Stanley lifted his head off his paws, blinking in confusion, before letting out a huge sigh and dropping his head back down with a *flump*.

'Seriously?' laughed Kate. 'You're going to sulk?'

She grabbed his lead from where she'd dumped it on the sofa the night before and rattled it at him. That did the trick. This time Stanley sat up, wiggling his eyebrows at her as if to say *Really? Not a trick like that time you took me to the V.E.T.?*

Kate patted her thigh. 'Walkies!' she said, then

laughed as he just blinked at her. 'Fine. If you're too tired, I'll just head down to the beach on my own. Bye.'

She took two steps out of the living room, and suddenly, there at her feet was a large bundle of fur, excitedly wagging his tail.

'Thought so!' she laughed.

The moment Stanley's paws hit the golden sand of West Beach, she knew he'd forgiven her for turfing him out of bed early. She snuggled down into her thick jumper and laughed as she watched him haring back and forth between her and the gentle, early morning waves as they lapped at the shore. It was the one place where he seemed to shrug off his slow-coach persona and turn into an absolute loon - a side of him she loved to see.

Considering how much Stanley hated having a bath - so much so that he never voluntarily entered the bathroom - it never ceased to amaze her how much he loved the sea. Watching as he pranced around in the shallows, leaping the little waves, she wondered whether Paula would be happy for him to join the Chilly Dippers for today's swim.

It had been a while since she'd taken him in for a proper dip and she didn't dare let him get into his stride right now without there being someone in the water with him ready to reign him in. Stanley had a habit of heading straight out into the open water, and she could really do without the added excitement of finding someone with a boat to go and fetch him this morning.

'Stanley!' she called sharply as he got in a bit deeper.

Stanley sloshed back out onto the beach, headed straight for her and promptly had a good shake.

'Gah! Thanks, you idiot!' she laughed, bending down to scruff his head as he bounded around, sending sand flying everywhere.

Kate straightened up, grinning. She'd been right about one thing - a good blast of early morning beach air was just what the doctor ordered. She'd managed to get herself in such a tizzy overnight but now, with the sky boasting that beautiful hazy glow that promised a scorching day ahead, and the fresh, salty breeze blowing through her hair, she felt braver, more sure of herself – and like she could take on any challenge.

'Come on Stanley, I've got an idea,' she muttered, turning her steps so that they were heading towards North Beach. 'Let's go suss out the competition before everyone else wakes up.'

They strode along the front, past the King's Nose and The Pebble Street Hotel, and then Kate led the way down the little stone steps onto the large grey pebbles of North Beach.

Stanley followed, his pace slowing as he picked his way over the trickier terrain. There was no doubt about it - he preferred West Beach for haring around like a nutter - but North Beach *definitely* had all the great smells.

He promptly scuttled over to investigate a barnacle-covered wooden boat that was pulled high up the beach, away from the tideline.

Kate highly doubted that it was sea-worthy anymore as it had been sitting here on the pebbles for months now - but Stanley loved it and every time they came down here he snuffled around underneath it, getting bits of seaweed stuck in his coat.

Kate trudged across the pebbles, making the most of the relative privacy of the beach to eye what would become the new frontage of New York Froth. It was pretty unlikely that there would be any locals around at this time of the morning to spot her on her recce, but still, she didn't much fancy becoming the main topic of conversation for the next couple of weeks.

Once she had a good view of the entire front of the old surf shop, Kate paused. There was no doubt about it – this was going to be a serious bit of competition for The Sardine when it opened up – no matter what she'd been trying to tell herself the day before.

For a start, this place would be able to seat so many more people. Probably fifty – perhaps even more if they were clever when it came to the new layout. The Sardine had space for eight... or maybe a dozen at a push – and that was with people perched all over the place.

Kate sighed, wrapped her arms protectively around

herself and chewed her lip. Serious, serious competition. Her original plan of staying the course and seeing what happened just wasn't going to cut it.

'Come on Stanley, let's go!' she clicked her fingers.

Stanley picked his way carefully back to her, but, at the last minute, Kate decided that she'd actually quite like a proper peep inside the empty shop – just so she knew what she was up against. There was no harm in that, was there? She wasn't doing anything wrong, even if someone *did* happen to spot her.

She climbed the steps up from North Beach and clipped Stanley's lead to his collar. With a quick look around her, she made her way across the road, around a couple of cars that were parked in the spaces outside and pressed her eye up against the window.

'It's bigger than I remember,' she muttered to Stanley, as he sat on her toes, panting. 'Gonna take him ages to sort out though – what a mess!'

She cupped her hands against the glass to get a better look. It was just a bare shell of a room, knackered, sun-bleached boarding on the walls with the occasional, empty clothes hanger, and some metal brackets that must have been used to hold up the surf boards for sale. It could be gorgeous – but boy, was it going to take some time – not to mention serious money – to get there.

'I don't think we've got anything to worry about for a couple of months. But still…'

Kate realised that she loved The Sardine way too

much to just sit back and "wait and see" if the arrival of New York Froth was going to have an effect. Sure, there wasn't anything she could do about it opening - but she *could* make sure her business was in the best possible shape to withstand the competition.

What she needed was something special, something unique that would set her apart from the crowd. Right now – she had her delivery round on Trixie and the amazing cakes Ethel made – but somehow, she didn't think that was going to be enough. She needed a plan. She owed it to her regulars. Hell, she owed it to herself.

'Checking out the competition?!'

The nasal, female voice made Kate jump back and she stumbled as she got tangled up with Stanley and his lead.

'Veronica!' she squeaked. 'You're up early!'

'Well... the early bird catches the worm and all that. So – you've heard the news about your new rivals then?' she said, raising an eyebrow and fixing a beady eye on Kate.

'I'd hardly call them rivals. We'll be catering to a very different bunch of customers.' She knew she sounded defensive, but she really had to make sure she didn't show a single sign of weakness in front of this woman – if she did, the news that she was closing down would be all around the town before it was even breakfast time.

Veronica laughed, though it wasn't a particularly joyful sound. 'Yeah, well – you're right about that. He'll be catering to the general public, and you'll be left with the dregs. Very different customers.'

Veronica paused and sniffed as she looked Kate up and down, a slight sneer on her face. 'Mark my words – things are starting to change for the better here in Seabury. More visitors, more money, more business. I'd advise you to move with the times – otherwise, The Sardine's just going to become a quaint memory.'

'Erm, okay. Thanks for that,' muttered Kate, taking a couple of steps away from Veronica as if the extra space between them would stop her from catching the woman's sceptical outlook on life.

Veronica shrugged. 'Just trying to help. I've been talking to the council. It's the businesses that move with the times they'll be supporting, you mark my words.'

Kate swallowed. She didn't really know what to say. There was "moving with the times" and then there was "destroying the spirit of Seabury". From what she knew of the local council, they tended to err on the side of destruction.

'Have a good day,' she said blandly, flashing Veronica a tight smile. She really did need to get away from her before she said something she'd regret.

'Oh, I will. Mike Pendle's taking me out to lunch later. He wants my advice - business person to business person, you know? We're going to that snazzy new place down in Plymouth – after all,' she paused for effect, 'it's not like there's anywhere decent here in Seabury, is there?'

Kate swallowed down a bitter retort then simply raised her hand in a half-hearted wave as she led Stanley away along the seafront as fast as his furry legs would go.

CHAPTER 6

'Wow – you're here early!' said Ethel, a note of worry in her voice as she bustled into the café.

Kate had watched her approach, then pause at the door with a look of surprise on her face. The fact that all the lights were already on, and the door was unlocked was a rare enough occurrence, but the fact that Kate was ensconced at one of the little tables with a bunch of paperwork strewn about in front of her had clearly been enough to startle her.

Kate smiled at Ethel. 'I'm making plans,' she said as if that explained everything.

'Plans? Going on holiday or something?'

'Nope. Plans for this place,' she said.

'Oh Kate – you're not selling, are you?' said Ethel, dumping the bags she was carrying down on the floor so that she could grasp the back of one of the chairs for support.

'Hell no!' laughed Kate. 'That's exactly why I'm making plans. Between you and me, I got myself all wound up about New York Froth last night. This morning I went down there to check it out – it's going to be massive.'

Ethel nodded. 'Yes, and I see he's already been in and papered over the windows. I guess he wants to do a big reveal when it's all ready.'

'You're kidding me?' said Kate, raising her eyebrows. 'Well, he's been in and done that in the past…' she glanced down at her battered old watch that had once belonged to her father, 'hour. And there I was thinking we'd have at least a couple of months before he got that place ready.'

'Oh, I expect you still do,' said Ethel, gathering her bags up and taking them over to the kitchen, ready to set out today's selection of delicacies. 'He'll need to hire the builders and the people to fit a new kitchen. And I'm sure there are all sorts of things he needs to sort out with the council before he's allowed to swap from being a shop to a café.'

'Something tells me he's probably got most of that in place already – and the bits he doesn't he will do soon. He's taking Veronica out to lunch, you know.'

'Well, if he's looking for advice from that old … *her*, then he's barking up the wrong tree, isn't he?!' growled Ethel.

Kate shrugged. 'In one way, maybe … but she does seem to know what the council wants and gets her way in most things eventually. Oh my - I bet that's why he's papered over the windows so quickly too. I was having a look in there first thing this morning and Veronica caught me. What's the betting she sent him a message the minute Stanley and I were out of sight?'

'Oh, I doubt she even waited that long,' muttered Ethel with a tut as she placed a dozen perfect fruity scones onto the top tier of a cake stand. 'Anyway – that's enough about her. Tell me about these plans of yours.'

'So far, the plan is to come up with a plan,' said Kate, shaking her head and shooting a sheepish grin at Ethel.

'Well, that's always a good start,' said Ethel with a heroic effort at keeping her face straight.

'Problem is – this place is tiny, it's not like I can expand without leaving here – which I'm *not* prepared to do. The delivery round covers everyone I can get to without taking a car instead of taking Trixie – which I'm *not* prepared to do…'

'Okay – I think I see the problem,' said Ethel.

'You do?'

She nodded. 'Yes – you're focusing on the negatives rather than the positives. Stop dwelling on the things you *don't* want to do and start thinking about the things you *could* do. Even better – the things you'd *like to do!*'

'So, you mean…'

'It's just a matter of a change of headspace and perspective. Rather than saying "I'm not prepared to give up Trixie" you might say... "I'm going to use Trixie to do special coffee and cake deliveries to events." She's quirky and good-looking enough to get into those selfie things, isn't she?!'

Kate stared at Ethel with her mouth open.

'Don't look at me like that. I use the inter webs too, you know.'

Kate grinned and shook her head. 'Sorry. Just a bit mind-blown here. I've sat struggling since silly o'clock and you've just handed me a suggestion in seconds.'

'All a matter of perspective. Don't narrow down your thinking too soon. List everything that you *could* do, then when you've thought as far outside the box as you can, start crossing things off the list.'

'I think you deserve a cup of coffee,' said Kate, leaping to her feet.

'Don't mind if I do,' said Ethel. 'Hey – where's Stanley?

'Down with the Chilly Dippers – Paula's taking him out for a swim. It was as much as I could do to stop him heading for France when we were down there earlier.'

'Bless his heart,' chuckled Ethel. 'I'm surprised Paula's going back in so soon after that funny turn she had though.'

Kate felt a sudden spike of anxiety hit her in the chest, and she busied herself loading the puck with freshly ground coffee, not wanting Ethel to catch the worry on her face.

'She's had some tests. She said she's feeling a lot better. Hopefully it was just a bit of an infection or something.'

Kate kept parroting this to herself whenever the image of Paula, looking pale and wan as she crashed to the floor of The Sardine a couple of weeks ago, flashed up in her mind. Kate had made her promise to go to the doctor, and Paula had been and got blood tests, but she swore it was nothing. Kate wasn't so sure. Her friend simply hadn't had the same bounce in her step for a while now.

Kate grabbed the milk jug and started to froth it as loudly as she could, just to buy herself a couple more seconds before she had to speak again.

'Here you go,' she said, placing the tall latte down in front of Ethel, and then gratefully accepting a cream and jam laden scone in return.

'Taste test,' laughed Ethel. It was a long-running joke.

Kate took a massive bite. There was nothing on earth as good as Ethel's scones … unless it was Ethel's Victoria sponge … or her flapjack.

'Yum!' said Kate. 'So, just going back to plans for this place for a second – there is one thing I definitely need to do straight away.'

Ethel nodded. 'New member of staff,' she said around a sip of coffee.

'Right. Because trying any bright new ideas will take at least one extra pair of hands.'

'Well – count me in too, won't you? And you never know – this new person might have some bright ideas of their own to throw into the mix.'

Kate nodded. She knew what Ethel was saying, but it would have to be someone really special before she'd trust them enough to bring them right into the heart of her little world so quickly.

'Come in, come in!' cried Kate, waving the mass of towel-clad women into the tiny café. 'Hands up for coffees?' she called, then quickly counted the raised hands. 'Teas? Anything else?'

'Hot chocolate times two.'

'Got any soup?'

'French onion,' called Ethel.

'Three please!'

It was always total bedlam when the Chilly Dippers piled in after a swim, and this morning was shaping up to be no exception. The windows steamed up in spite of the warmer weather outside, as much vigorous towel-drying, hair wringing and wrangling of warm post-swim hoodies and sweatpants took place.

'Hello boy, did you behave?' said Kate, patting Stanley's head as he trundled over to say hello, then promptly regretting it as he was drenched and covered in sand.

'He was as good as gold. Only one attempt at seal-watching,' laughed Paula, leading the soggy doggy back out of the kitchen and treating him to a vigorous rub down with the towel that Kate always had on hand for him.

'Thanks so much!' said Kate, peeping at her friend while she was busy, and letting out a secret sigh of relief to see that Paula was flushed from her swim and looking much happier and healthier than she had done in a while.

'We love having him! He's our honorary member, you know that.'

Kate grinned. She loved the fact that the locals were as much of a family to Stanley as they were to her. She really did live in the best place in the entire world.

'Oh - by the way,' said Kate, carrying a tray laden with hot drinks into the middle of the gaggle of damp women - who pounced as if their lives depended on wrapping their cold fingers around the warm mugs - 'if anyone's looking for a job, or knows of anyone who'd like to work here – I'm looking to find a replacement for Claire.'

'Have you got any fliers or anything? I can pass some around work for you,' said Paula.

Kate shook her head. 'I don't – but I could easily print some up before I deliver to you guys later?'

'Perfect!' said Paula.

Kate grinned at her friend. She worked in a large graphic design company on the outskirts of town... and Paula knew everyone.

'Drop some in to me too, love,' said Doreen, who owned the post office. 'I'll display some in the shop, and pop some in with the local paper deliveries too if you'd like?'

'Yes please!' said Kate, her heart filling with warmth. As usual, the people of Seabury were rushing to her aid. She made a mental note that both Doreen and Paula were on free coffees for the rest of the week.

'How'd it go?' asked Ethel as Kate and Stanley strode back into the café, Kate slightly breathless after what had felt like a particularly arduous sandwich round. Maybe when she found the new person, they'd be up for doing it occasionally, just to give her legs a break!

'Yeah – not too bad,' she said, having nodded a greeting to the half a dozen regulars who'd pulled the two tables together and were sitting in one big group, munching on tea cakes.

'They take the fliers?' asked Ethel.

'Yeah – that was no problem. I just don't know if it's going to work – you know how picky I am.'

'I do. But that's not a reason to start discounting people before you've even met them,' laughed Ethel.

'The right person will come along, just you wait and see. I bet it's the last person on earth you'd expect, too.'

'You're probably right. Busy here?' asked Kate. It had really lifted her flagging spirits to come back to find the outdoor tables playing host to a whole gaggle of cyclists. Maybe she really did need to get over her dislike for visitors. After all, if she didn't live here herself, she'd definitely want to visit – take a holiday close to the sea and suck in all the beauty Seabury had to offer.

'Very busy here,' said Ethel.

Kate beamed. 'Not too much for you?'

'Course not,' said Ethel stoutly. 'Though I'm not pretending I won't be glad when you've got someone new to help take up the slack… I'll be falling behind on my cake baking and jam duties otherwise!'

'Can't have that!' said Kate, taking Ethel's hand and giving it a quick squeeze. 'But thank you. Really. I don't know what I'd have done without you. And I'm not just talking about these past few weeks, either.'

'Get away with you girl!' said Ethel, giving her a friendly swipe on the arm and then feeling around in her apron pocket to give Stanley a treat.

Kate watched them fondly for a moment, a smile on her face. Ethel had been there as long as she could remember. She'd been her babysitter when her dad had needed a rare bit of grown-up time. She'd been there when Kate got a bit older and needed a female perspective. And now, here she was – still taking care of her, looking out for her, being her friend.

'Excuse me? Are you Kate Hardy?'

Kate spun around, turning slightly pink at being caught in the middle of such an unguarded moment. She usually kept a tight lid on her treasured memories – they were only to be pulled out and looked at in the sanctuary of her flat when she was alone.

'Yep. That's me,' she said, smiling at the young girl who'd materialised in front of her. 'What can I do for you?'

'Well ... I wanted to ask about this,' she said, waving one of Kate's recently printed fliers. 'Is the job still up for grabs?'

Kate had to force herself not to laugh. 'Erm – very much so. I only handed those out about an hour ago.'

'Ah, brilliant!' grinned the girl.

'Hey – didn't I spot you in here yesterday?' said Kate, suddenly recognising the young face as the girl who'd sat outside in the afternoon and had steadily worked her way through three pots of tea and sampled every single cake they had on offer.

She nodded and smiled. 'So ... I don't know what experience you're after?' she asked. Clearly she wasn't going to be derailed from her purpose.

'Well...' said Kate slowly. This girl looked to be quite a bit younger than she'd normally go for, but she had to be careful, she didn't want to crush her outright.

'I do need some decent experience in a café or something similar.'

'That's no problem – I've worked on and off at one every school holiday for the last two years where I used to live.'

'Are you new in town?' asked Kate, though in reality she already knew the answer – after all, she quite literally knew *everyone* in town, and she didn't recognise this girl's face – yesterday was the first time she'd set eyes on her.

'Yep. Just moved here. I'm Sarah, by the way,' she thrust a hand out for Kate to shake. Kate had to bite her lip to stop herself from letting out a giggle at the firm grasp.

'Well, it's really lovely to meet you, Sarah. So, do you mind if I ask how old you are?'

Sarah shrugged. 'Course not. I'm sixteen,' she said, glancing back over her shoulder towards the door.

'So you're still at school?' asked Kate, wondering who the girl was looking for.

She shook her head and turned her attention back to Kate. 'I finished my GCSEs at my old school. Now I'm here, I really want to go to college, but dad's being a prat about it – he says I have to take A levels and go to university.'

'And what do you want to do?'

'Bake,' said Sarah. 'I want to go to college and do a course that means I can train up as... I don't know... maybe a pastry chef?'

'Wow,' said Kate. She couldn't help but be impressed by the girl's ambition and the fact that she knew what she wanted to do at such a young age. 'Thing is, no matter if you go to school or to college – I really need someone who can work some weekdays for me too…'

'Oh…' Sarah chewed her lip and looked around her for a moment. 'Well – I wouldn't be starting back until September no matter what happens. If I get my way and go to college – it won't be full time, so I could do some weekdays with you – especially if you'd let me learn some of the baking. I might be able to count it towards the course then.'

Kate's mind was racing. She knew she shouldn't be jumping into anything too quickly, and the girl was so far from the ideal candidate it wasn't even funny… but she was getting a weirdly good feeling about her. Still, she needed a few seconds to think.

'Morning Kate!'

Kate glanced around to find one of her regulars waiting to be served.

'Sorry Mary!' she said quickly. 'Your usual?'

'Please! And a teacake. I'll be outside.'

Kate turned to Sarah. 'You used a coffee machine before?'

'Of course!' said Sarah, looking hopeful.

'Well, ours in ancient, Italian, and particularly temperamental. Two lattes – one for Ethel, one for me, and Mary will have a cappuccino. Let's see what you've got!'

Sarah plonked her bag down excitedly on one of the stools and pulled the sleeves of her long black tee-shirt up a bit before moving around to join Ethel on the other side of the counter – where she stopped dead.

'Oh my goodness!' she gasped.

'Okay, dear?' asked Ethel, raising a quick eyebrow at Kate.

Sarah dropped to her knees in front of Stanley and held out the back of her hand for him to sniff – he did so and then promptly gave it a great big lick, making Sarah laugh.

'What a sweetheart!' she said, stroking his head. 'Is he yours?' she looked up at Ethel.

'Kate's.'

'Ah – good point,' said Kate. 'Sarah – meet Stanley. If I'm here, he's here. So, being around him kinda goes with the job…' she said, watching Sarah closely for her reaction.

'Bonus!' said Sarah, beaming at her. 'Right. Sorry,' she got to her feet looking a bit embarrassed. 'Sorry,' she said again. 'I love dogs – I've always wanted one but … parents, you know?'

Kate grinned at her and nodded. This was looking more and more promising by the second.

She watched as Sarah moved to the sink and thoroughly washed her hands before drying them on some blue paper from the dispenser and moving over to the Italian Stallion. She looked so at home in the cramped kitchen, careful not to stand on Stanley or bump into

Ethel as she went, that Kate could swear she'd already been working there for several months.

Now came real the test. There were very few people who could get that coffee machine to work with them rather than against them. Kate loved it – but it had taken both Ethel and Claire quite a while to learn its little foibles.

A minute later, Kate was looking down into a latte that looked just about perfect – especially as it had an absolutely adorable little bird swirled into the milk.

She took a sip with her eyes closed. Okay, it was official – if she hired this girl, she could retire from coffee making duties forever. Sarah not only had the knack – this coffee was better than the ones she made herself.

Kate didn't make a comment but instead opened her eyes to watch as Ethel took a sip of her own coffee. She raised her eyebrows and nodded her approval to Kate. Sarah didn't notice – she was fastidiously cleaning the steam spout and emptying the coffee puck ready for the next customer.

'Can you take Mary's out too?' she asked.

'Course!' said Sarah, gathering up the scone Ethel had prepared and scooting outside.

She reappeared with a smile. 'Mary's nice!' she said.

'Okay, Sarah – here's the thing…' started Kate.

'Uh oh,' said Sarah, suddenly looking nervous. 'Not the thing. The thing's never good, is it?!'

Kate chuckled.

'I'll do a trial, or I'll even work just to help you out until you find someone more permanent – whatever you need!'

Kate held up her hand and Sarah promptly put her hand over her mouth to stop herself from talking.

'How about we start by calling it a summer job? Work with me until September – then we'll figure out what's what?' she asked.

Sarah's lip quivered and for a moment. Kate thought she was going to burst into tears, but then she seemed to get control over whatever emotion she was grappling with and she nodded. 'Sounds perfect to me. When do I start?'

'How does tomorrow sound?'

Sarah reached out and shook Kate's hand again, then squatted down next to Stanley, who'd wandered over to sniff her trainers. 'You and me are going to be best friends!' she said, wrapping her arms around him in a giant hug.

CHAPTER 7

Kate passed the turning to the lighthouse and stopped for a brief moment to stare lovingly at her favourite spot. She'd like nothing more right now than to take a few minutes to sit there with Stanley and stare quietly out to sea – but today definitely wasn't the day for it. She needed to get back to The Sardine and take over the Sarah-sitting duties from Ethel.

The young girl had only been with them a few days, but Kate was pretty sure that she could already run the place all by herself whilst blindfolded if she needed to. Not only was she incredibly capable and soaking up every bit of new information like a sponge, but she'd also fitted in as if she'd been there for years. The customers seemed to like her, Lionel had given her his seal of approval, and she and Ethel had already become firm friends.

Kate loved how eager she was to learn. Sure, she was more than a little bit reserved when it came to talking about her home life and parents, but Kate wasn't going to push her on that – all in good time. She would rather that The Sardine was a sanctuary Sarah could count on if she needed it. After all, she could still just about remember how tricky being a teenager was!

In fact, as far as Kate could see, Sarah's age was the only drawback in the whole equation. She and Ethel had agreed that Sarah wasn't to be left to work alone – it wasn't that she wouldn't be able to handle it, but Kate would hate for anything to happen – whether a burn from the Italian Stallion or a run-in with one of the more stubborn customers who sometimes stumbled into their little world.

Kate wanted to make sure that Sarah would *always* have back-up if she needed it. After all – she *was* only sixteen.

To begin with, Kate had worried that this meant they were still at square one. After all, it was an extra person to pay, and it didn't give her or Ethel any more freedom to take time out than they'd had before Sarah had started. On top of that, she'd *still* need to hire someone else. But Kate quickly changed her tune. Sarah had already helped her to pack up the orders and load Trixie each day – giving Kate more time to focus on the customers in the café and Ethel more time to do some extra baking.

Suddenly, between the three of them, it felt like they

might actually get some time to come up with some new plans to keep New York Froth off their backs.

In fact, it was the first thing she was going to do when she got back, before Ethel left for the day – arrange a bit of a staff get-together to pick their brains – the sooner the better!

With one last look out across the lighthouse and a quick check that Stanley was still sitting comfortably, Kate pushed off and freewheeled along until she was hurtling down the steep hill back into the heart of Seabury.

As she whizzed past, she couldn't help but notice how many of the outlying cottages had either been converted into B&Bs or holiday homes. In fact, she passed Stanley's old place on this part of her route - now a second home to some rich city types who only visited about three times a year.

Kate had always made it her policy not to deliver to the second homes and air B&Bs. She hated that the housing prices around here sky-rocketed because a bunch of rich idiots wanted a country bolthole for the occasional weekend. It had practically broken her heart when she'd had to sell her dad's house after he'd passed away. There had been no way that she could afford to take on the mortgage for such a large place. But the thing that really stuck in her throat was that it was now owned by someone who used it maybe two days a month at most.

Kate took a deep breath and shook her head so that

the wind whipped through her hair as she tried to let go of her anger. Something good had come of it, after all. The swift sale had meant that she'd been able to buy The Sardine and her flat. But now... now that it came to shoring up the café against this new threat, perhaps it was time to swallow her pride - and her prejudice - for the sake of everything she held dear.

As usual, Kate slowed as she trundled into the heart of the town - passing *Nana's*, the little ice-cream parlour that had been going for as long as she could remember. Hm. Maybe that's where she should take Ethel and Sarah. What better way to get the creative juices flowing than a double cone with a good sprinkling of chopped nuts, or hundreds and thousands, or her personal favourite - hot fudge sauce?

Yes - they'd make a date, she'd cook for them and then they'd go out and take in the sights. After all, Seabury itself was the best muse she knew.

Letting out a little sigh of relief to find Trixie's yard wasn't blocked this morning, Kate indicated and pedalled the tricycle through the open gates. Then she hopped off, helped Stanley out of the trailer and loaded her arms with the empty bags and boxes from yet another successful delivery round.

'Need a hand?'

Sarah appeared at the entrance to the yard, and quickly took the stack of massive Tupperware tubs out of Kate's arms so that she could grab the last few bits from Trixie's trailer.

'Thanks Sarah!' said Kate gratefully.

'No probs - we saw you pull up. Round go okay?'

Kate nodded. She was wiped.

'Come on - I'll make you a coffee. Me and Ethel have tried out a new shortbread recipe for you to taste test!'

Kate's ears pricked up at this. 'Sounds good! Has it been quiet then?'

Sarah shook her head, expertly balancing the boxes with one arm while she opened the café door for them both with the other. 'Nope - it's been heaving. There's a bunch of new what-ya-call ems... erm... you know, *moth guys?*'

Kate snorted. 'We need a sign - "Moth Guys welcome here!"'

Sarah stuck out her tongue. 'You know what I mean!'

Kate nodded, chuckling as she made her way into the café and plonked her armload down onto the counter.

Sarah went straight over to the Italian Stallion to make Kate a coffee while her boss slumped into one of the chairs.

'Some days that hill out of town is a bit much for these old legs!' she sighed.

'You could always drive?' said Sarah, peeping back over her shoulder as she loaded the puck.

'Wash your mouth out!' said Kate with a grin.

Sarah rolled her eyes.

'I know I need to make some changes around here if we're going to be able to compete with the new boy, but that's not one of them.'

'It would be a lot faster – and you could go further-' said Ethel, in a gentle voice.

Kate stared at her, knowing full well that she'd never suggest such a thing if there wasn't the protection of the counter between them.

'Nope. Trixie stays. Our customers love her – and I might complain, but I love her too. Anyway – Stanley'd never forgive me.'

'Well …' said Sarah slowly, popping a perfect cappuccino down in front of Kate along with a piece of shortbread, 'if Trixie's staying, maybe you could make her work a bit harder for you?' said Sarah.

'How'd you mean?' asked Kate curiously.

Sarah shrugged. 'Not sure – but she *is* kind of your mascot. Everyone knows her, but she's hidden in the yard all day. Maybe you could use her as a bit of advertising somehow – a way to bring new customers in. Or, I don't know, visit events with her or something?'

Kate nodded slowly. 'Yeah... Ethel suggested events too...' This was exactly what she needed – fresh ideas that weren't weighed down with years and years of "this is how I've always done it".

'Okay, you two – I'd like to cook a meal for you both. A kind of mini team-party.'

'Ooh,' said Ethel. 'That sounds lovely. I could bring a trifle!'

Kate grinned. Ethel never went anywhere empty-handed. 'How about Sunday afternoon – are you both free? We'll be closed here, so that makes it easier…'

'I'd love that!' said Sarah, looking thrilled to be included.

'Brilliant! Though I have to warn you that I've got an ulterior motive – I'm going to pick your brains remorselessly.'

'About…?' said Sarah.

'This place. It's time to shake things up a bit, and the only way we're going to do that is as a team.'

Sarah bounced excitedly.

'Oh – by the way Sarah, can you give me a number for your parents? Just so I can check it's okay with them?'

Sarah instantly stopped bouncing. 'I … erm … they'll be totally fine with it.'

'Okay,' said Kate, a bit taken aback. 'But I do need a number anyway – just for an *in case of emergency* contact, you know? I've got a form and because you're under eighteen, I'd prefer it if they could sign it and let me know how best to contact them.'

She watched as Sarah chewed her lip for a second, trying to hide her face as she started to wipe down the already immaculate counter. There was something else going on here, but maybe now, in the middle of the shift wasn't the best time to push it.

She glanced at Ethel to see if she'd picked up on anything, and her old friend instantly met her eye and raised a worried eyebrow. Uh oh – so it wasn't just her.

'What time on Sunday?' said Ethel to break the silence.

'I was thinking about five? We can eat early, throw some ideas around and then I'll treat you both to whatever you fancy from Nana's before they close?'

Sarah looked over at her and Kate was relieved to see a grin on her face. 'Perfect!'

Kate grabbed one of the tables and hauled it towards the doors of The Sardine. She'd already sent Sarah home at three as she'd been there so early that morning. Kate could tell she was going to have her hands full with Sarah – but in the very best way. The customers adored her, and the young girl was so keen that it was practically impossible to make her take a break, let alone send her home at the end of her shifts.

Heading back outside for the other table, Kate wondered again about what the story with her parents was. She never talked about them, had shaken her head when she'd asked if she had any brothers or sisters, and Kate had found the 'In Case of Emergency' form she'd printed off abandoned in the kitchen after she'd left.

For whatever reason, Sarah really didn't want Kate to have anything to do with them ... and she really didn't feel comfortable about that.

She pulled her mobile out of her pocket, intending to give Ethel a quick call. If she couldn't get Sarah to open up, perhaps Ethel might have more luck.

Just as she pulled up Ethel's number, her screen started flashing with an incoming call.

Kate grinned and ran her fingers through her tousled mop of hair as she answered and slumped down into the last chair left out on the pavement.

'Hello Kate.'

'Pierre!' she grinned. 'I haven't heard from you in forever!'

'I am sorry, ma chérie, it has been busy – for you too, yes?'

'Definitely!' laughed Kate.

'But – are you free ce soir?'

Was she free tonight? Hell yes! She couldn't imagine a better way to finish the day.

'Absolutely!'

'In… un heur?'

'Perfect!'

'I only stay one night. Tomorrow I must go back home.'

'Then we'd better make it count!' said Kate with a huge smile.

CHAPTER 8

Kate rolled over in her bed and reached a hand out, searching for the smooth warmth of Pierre's skin. Instead, all she found were rumpled sheets that were already cold. Shit – had she overslept?

She sat bolt upright and reached for the little alarm clock that sat on her bedside table. Six forty-five in the morning. Huh. So, where the hell was Pierre? Maybe he'd been unable to sleep and had decamped down to the living room so that he didn't disturb her... not that there would be much chance of him doing that after they'd finally curled up to sleep so late the night before!

After getting his call, Kate had hurried to lock up The Sardine, packed a massive picnic basket full of tasty leftovers, and then ran upstairs for a hasty shower. She'd even managed to add a quick slick of mascara and lip-gloss before the sound of the doorbell was met with Stanley's eager, booming bark.

Much to Stanley's disgust, Kate had whisked Pierre off for a romantic stroll, leaving him with an order to stay put in his bed. She did feel a bit bad about it – after all, Stanley was usually with her no matter what was going on - but this was different. He definitely wouldn't have been a good addition for what she had planned.

Kate had led Pierre to one of the secret coves just along from West Beach. She'd discovered this particular one when she was a teenager and had never yet met a single soul there when she visited. This might have been something to do with the fact that you had to scramble along a practically hidden path through a thicket of brambles and blackthorn, and then clamber down a steep, muddy cliff on your behind to get there – but boy, was it worth it.

Golden sand and the perfect, private place for skinny dipping. She and Pierre had made the most of it, and she thanked her lucky stars that she'd remembered to pack her tartan picnic blanket.

Kate rolled out of bed and snagged her silky robe off the floor where it had been unceremoniously tossed away by Pierre the night before. Slipping it on, she listened for any sounds in the flat, but everything was completely quiet.

She padded across to the bathroom, hastily wiped the smudged mascara from under her eyes (no point terrifying the poor guy!) and then silently made her way downstairs. She peeped into the kitchen, which was empty, then pushed open the door and made her way into the living room.

Stanley lifted his head from his bed and wagged his tail. At least it looked like he'd forgiven her for abandoning him the night before. But there was no sign of her visitor.

'Where's he got to then, Stan?' she said, bending low to tickle his ears.

Stanley let out a huge sigh and flopped back down onto his bed. His meaning was more than clear – he couldn't give a monkeys what had happened to the interloper that had cost him his evening walk!

Kate straightened up and went back through to the kitchen. As she was up, she may as well grab a cup of tea. She went to flick the kettle on and paused. There on the counter was a folded piece of paper with her name on the front. She grabbed it and unfolded the sheet that looked like it had been torn from the pad she used for her shopping lists.

Ma Cherie Kate,

Merci! I had an amazing time with you. Désolé. So sorry I have to leave early. I did not want to wake you – you need your sleep after last night! I closed the door so the dog did not follow me out. See you next time.

Pierre x

. . .

Kate stared at the note and for just a moment, a little wave of disappointment ran through her. Then she let out a sigh, popped the piece of paper in the bin and flicked the kettle on. She didn't have the right to be disappointed. This was how things were between them. It was what she *wanted*, wasn't it? They'd had a wonderful evening – and it was too much to expect breakfast together before he disappeared back to France, wasn't it? Anyway, she needed to get a wiggle on if she wanted to turn all the fish he'd brought her from his boat into a pie in time for the lunchtime crowd!

~

'Oh my God, what's that amazing smell?' said Sarah, bowling into The Sardine with a Tupperware box clamped under one arm, followed closely by Ethel.

'Fish pie,' said Kate.

'Ah yes, the smell of a visit from a certain Frenchman,' laughed Ethel.

'Oi!' said Kate, letting out a laugh.

'You don't have to pretend it's not true,' said Ethel, eyeing her sternly. 'One look at that glow on your face and anyone could tell what you've been up to!'

'Ethel!' laughed Sarah in delight, turning to stare at her.

'What? I may be old, young lady, but I'm not past it.'

'Wouldn't dream of saying you were! Anyway – when do I get to meet the guy?' Sarah demanded.

'What? Kate's guy? You'll be lucky!' laughed Ethel. 'That man's like quicksand. I think I caught a glimpse in passing ... maybe once?'

Kate shrugged. 'He's busy.'

'That's one way of putting it. I'm guessing he was gone before you even woke up this morning?'

Kate shrugged.

'Nothing changes,' sighed Ethel.

'That sucks,' said Sarah. 'How come you look so happy?' she said, turning back to Kate.

'Because I like things just the way they are,' she said decidedly. 'Anyway you two, enough of all that! What's in the box Sarah?'

'An experiment. I wondered if you'd let me know what you think?'

'And so it begins,' laughed Ethel.

'You don't have to!' said Sarah, looking a bit embarrassed.

'Oh, no lass, don't misunderstand me. You're just reminding me of myself. And Kate here too – when she started experimenting with pie fillings.'

'Oh!' said Sarah, looking between the two of them.

'Yeah – welcome to the club!' said Kate. 'And gimmie! I could do with a pick-me-up before I head out.'

Sarah opened the box almost shyly as Kate strode over to join her and Ethel at the counter.

'Oh my,' breathed Ethel.

'Holy mackerel!' said Kate.

'I think you mean holy macarons, actually!' chuckled Ethel. 'May I?'

Sarah nodded, looking decidedly nervous.

Ethel reached in and gently lifted out one of the delicacies. Apple-shaped, the macaron was a rich red colour and glazed in a shiny red coating. A stalk crafted of chocolate stuck out of the side, a tiny leaf piped on in green icing.

'I hate to do this, but...' Ethel broke it in half to reveal a perfect, gooey centre. She popped half in her mouth and chewed.

Kate and Sarah stared at her, following her every move as if she was a *Bake Off* judge.

'Oh my!' she groaned.

'Right, my turn!' said Kate, nabbing one for herself and taking a bite.

'Cinnamon and apple?' she breathed.

Sarah nodded. 'Do you like it?'

'Mmmmmmm!' chorused the two women together.

'Alright back there, boy?' she called to Stanley over her shoulder as she pumped her legs for all she was worth, heading up the hill out of Seabury to her first stop on

WELCOME TO SEABURY

the sandwich round – the graphic design company where Paula worked.

Stanley seemed to grin at her from his perch, looking as happy as Larry. Kate laughed and stood up on the pedals to give her a bit of extra oomph to get to the top road.

Hearing a car coming up behind them, Kate kept pedalling as hard as she could. This part of the road was ridiculously narrow, and there would be no chance they could overtake here - but she knew that there was a decent passing spot she could pull into about fifty meters ahead. She started to pant with the extra effort. Not long now and she'd be out of their way.

Whoever was behind them started to impatiently rev their engine, making Stanley bark. Kate threw a cross look over her shoulder and swore. The car was mere feet behind Trixie, deliberately tailgating her, pulling closer then dropping back, then pulling even closer again. Kate squinted, but the light reflecting off the windscreen meant that she couldn't make out the driver's face.

Stanley was now on his feet, barking his head off, and there was quite literally nothing Kate could do because the prick wasn't even giving her enough space to slow down, let alone stop.

Letting a fluent stream of swear words flow from her lips as she pumped her legs even harder, Kate did her best to keep up the pace, heading as fast as she could for the pull-in and praying that Stanley didn't get so freaked out that he tried to do anything stupid.

The road started to widen slightly. Kate could just about see the pull-in up ahead when the driver decided that they couldn't wait any longer and swerved to the right, determined to overtake.

'What the hell?!' squealed Kate, steering Trixie in towards the spikey, thorned hedge on the left.

The huge estate car whizzed alongside her, coming so close that she had to wrench the handlebars and steer them right off the road onto the verge in an attempt to stop the car from clipping their side. The handlebars juddered and jerked in Kate's hands. Trixie's front wheel hit a rock and Kate fell off the saddle just as the trailer toppled onto its side.

'Stanley!' Kate screamed, scrambling on hands and knees around the back.

Stanley cowered away from her, backing in towards the hedge.

'It's okay boy, you're okay,' she crooned, her voice shaking with the shock of what had just happened. She managed to lay one hand gently on his head and get hold of his collar with the other. He let out a little whimper - a sound she might expect from a puppy rather than her great big bear of a dog.

'Don't be hurt, don't be hurt!' she muttered, stroking him and trying to coax him forwards out of the hedge a bit. She really needed to get Trixie fully off of the road, but she didn't dare let go of Stanley in case he bolted in fright.

'Here,' she said reaching into her pocket with her free hand. 'Biscuit?'

Stanley's nose twitched and he moved closer to her to snaffle the treat. Kate groaned. There was no mistaking the fact that he was limping and trying to carry his front foot.

Kate did her best not to panic. The last thing she wanted to do was stress Stanley out even more. She reached into her cardigan pocket where she'd stashed the rope lead she always carried with her and gently clipped it onto his collar, then carefully stood up. *She* didn't seem to have hurt herself in the fall - at least that was something.

'Can you walk?' she said, trying to coax Stanley forward. She really did need to get Trixie out of this narrow part of the road before this disaster turned into something even messier.

Stanley stood up, took two limping steps and then promptly sat back down with a little whine.

'Oh, my poor baby!' she said, fighting back tears as shock started to set in. 'I'm going to kill that...'

She drew her mobile out of her pocket. Thankfully it was unscathed. She needed to call for some help. She was just about to dial The Sardine's number when she heard the sounds of an approaching engine. Balls!

She was just about to try yanking the trailer to see if

she could slide it sideways when a white pick-up crawled into view.

'Kate love! What's happened?!'

Charlie's kind, worried face appeared alongside her, staring at her out of the window.

Kate felt her lip wobble as tears that were part-rage and part-shock threatened to spill over.

'It's okay, it's okay love. We'll get you sorted.'

Charlie popped the truck's hazard lights on and killed the engine. He hopped quickly down and made his way around to Kate.

'Did you crash?' he said in surprise.

Kate shook her head. 'Stanley's hurt!' was all she managed to force out around the massive lump of fear in her throat.

'Bleeding?' he asked quickly, bending down and stroking Stanley's head.

Kate shook her head. 'It's his front leg. It... it might be broken.'

'Okay. First things first. Come on lad.'

Charlie wrapped his arms around Stanley and with surprising strength, lifted him gently in his arms. Stanley let out a little yelp that turned into a pathetic whine. The sound nearly finished Kate off - but she just about managed to hold it together enough to open the truck's passenger door. Charlie gently placed Stanley in the footwell on top of what looked to be a fleece jacket.

'Let's get Trixie in the back - we can look at her later. We need to get the lad straight to the vet.'

Between them, they unhooked the little trailer from Trixie and managed to haul her into the open back of the truck.

'Right,' said Charlie. 'Let's go.'

Kate nodded, pursing her lips as she climbed up into the passenger seat, careful not to nudge Stanley with her foot.

'It's okay boy,' she said, gently stroking his head. 'You'll be okay.'

'What happened?' asked Charlie as he pulled out onto the top road.

'We got pushed off the road by a car,' said Kate, doing her best not to growl.

'What? That's terrible! And they didn't even stop?!'

'No,' said Kate, struggling to keep a lid on her anger as she fully realised this fact for the first time. 'No, he bloody well didn't, did he?'

'He? So you know who it was?'

Kate nodded. It had been the same estate car that had blocked Trixie's yard just the other day. 'That car belongs to Mike bloody Pendle.'

CHAPTER 9

'Are you okay?'
'Where's Stanley?'
'What exactly happened?'
'You've been gone for hours!'

Kate was greeted back into The Sardine by a barrage of worried questions from Ethel and Sarah. She'd called them from the vet's and told them there had been an accident. Ethel had agreed to call all her customers, but there hadn't been time to give her the ins and outs of what had happened. It had been as much as Kate could do not to dissolve into a puddle of tears on the phone. If she was honest, she wasn't far off it now, either.

'That Mike Pendle ran her off the road in his car,' said Charlie, a frown marring his usually smiling face as he followed her in and, seeing that the café was empty – it being long after the lunchtime rush by this point – shut the door firmly behind him and flipped the sign to "closed".

'*What?!*' squeaked Sarah, the colour draining from her face. 'But he *couldn't* have. I mean...' she paused, looking a bit like she was going to fall over. She looked to Ethel for some kind of support, but the older woman gave a little shrug and shook her head.

'Hang on, where's Stanley?' Sarah demanded. 'Oh my God. He's not...?'

Kate sank into one of the empty chairs. 'We had to leave him at the vet's. He needs an x-ray. He might have a broken leg – though the vet thinks it's probably just sprained. But she wants to check there's nothing else going on that we can't see.'

'Oh no, poor lad,' said Ethel, shaking her head, and bringing a cup of tea over to Kate. 'Charlie, what can I get for you?'

'Oh, nothing thanks,' he said, smiling at her warmly. 'I'll just get out of your hair.'

'Please Charlie, I insist!' said Kate, indicating for him to sit down with her. 'I've wasted your entire day running around after me like that.'

'Not wasted. I'm glad to help,' he mumbled.

'You're our hero, coming to the rescue like that!' said Ethel, her voice soft.

'Oh I don't know about that...' he said scratching his nose and turning red.

'You are!' said Sarah. 'Imagine if you hadn't come along!'

'I don't want to think about that, thanks,' said Kate, doing her best to suppress a shudder. 'Did you guys manage to call everyone?' she asked as Sarah hovered over her and Charlie while Ethel bustled off to make him a drink.

Sarah nodded. 'Ethel got straight on the phone to everyone – she worked through your delivery list and explained you'd had an accident and were stuck at the vet's.'

'Many complaints?'

'Are you mad?' said Ethel from the kitchen. 'Everyone was just worried about you and Stanley!'

'But no one got their deliveries,' she sighed.

'Most of them put in a new order over the phone and sent someone down to collect it. We nearly ran out of cake, so we sold all of Sarah's macarons too. Paula came down from their lot and even took some deliveries up to a couple of places that couldn't make it down into town themselves.'

Kate shook her head and tried to control the wave of emotion that ran through her. As usual, the kindness of the locals amazed her. Well – *most* locals. 'That must have been bedlam for you guys!'

'Busy, but it was okay – Sarah was amazing,' said Ethel, unable to hide the note of pride in her voice.

'Thank you both so much. I don't know what I'd do

without you two. I think I'll have to make something special to take everyone when I get back to the round next week… you know, a little apology…'

'Next week?' said Sarah, sounding worried.

Kate shrugged. 'Luckily it's Saturday tomorrow, so no round anyway. Closed on Sunday. And maybe - hopefully - Trixie'll be fixed up by Monday… though I'm not sure how likely that is…'

'Oh no! Trixie's broken too?' said Ethel.

Charlie nodded. 'Needs a bit of straightening out after her tumble, that's all. I'm sure she'll be okay.'

'You know, Kate love, I think maybe we should shut up shop for the rest of the day. Or at least, you should take the afternoon off,' said Ethel, popping a small pile of post down in front of Kate and perching on the chair next to her for a moment. 'I don't mind working with Sarah until closing time. You've had a shock and you'll be worrying about Stanley until you know what's happening. The last thing you need to be doing is fielding customers.'

Kate started to shake her head, but fear about Stanley combined with bone-tired weariness made her want to curl up and go to sleep instead. She wasn't sure what to say, so she picked up the top envelope from the pile just for something to do and slit it open.

'You know, Ethel's right,' said Charlie.

'But… then he'll win!' muttered Kate, drawing the letter out.

'Who?'

'Mike Pendle. I can't let him win.'

'Love,' said Ethel in a gentle tone, 'I don't think he did it on purpose. Yes, it was irresponsible and awful, but there's no way…'

'You didn't see what he was doing,' growled Kate.

'Well, no…'

'He wouldn't do that,' said Sarah in a decided voice.

'Well,' said Kate, trying to keep her calm, 'I'm afraid he did.'

'Actually,' said Sarah, there's something I need to talk to you about. Well, something I need to tell you…'

Kate looked up just in time to see Ethel shake her head quickly at Sarah. 'Maybe another time, love,' she said, a firm note to her voice. 'Kate's had a bit of a shock.'

'No, it's okay Sarah,' said Kate. 'Just give me a couple of minutes to land and go through this lot first and then…' she trailed off, glancing down at the piece of paper in her hand. 'Son of a b-!'

'What?' said Ethel, her eyebrows raised.

Kate looked up again to find all three of them staring at her in concern. She took a deep breath, trying to steady herself, trying to keep the well of anger that was building in her chest from breaking loose.

'You know what,' she said, her voice hard and low. 'I think I'll take you up on that offer of an afternoon off.'

'Good idea,' said Sarah, sounding relieved. 'Maybe a bath and…'

Kate shook her head. 'I'm going to go and pay Mike

Pendle a visit. This,' she said, shaking the letter like she was trying to wring its neck, 'this means war!'

~

Kate hammered on the locked and papered door of the old surf shop. She was shaking from head to toe as pure, unadulterated rage coursed through her veins.

Where the hell was he, the conniving, tailgating, backstabbing...?

Kate banged on the door again, this time with both fists. She knew she should cool off, try to get into a calmer state of mind and think this through so that she could approach it rationally. She *knew* that she looked a bit like a rabid dog right now but-

'Mike Pendle!' she yelled. 'Get your arse out here *right* now!'

She knew there were people working in there. She could hear a radio and see shadows moving around behind the paper. It struck her, somewhere in the tiny part of her brain that was still clinging onto sanity, that Mike might not actually be here at all - but she ignored that thought. He *had* to be here.

She was just about to hammer again when there was the sound of a key being turned, then the door cracked open.

'Who the hell are you?'

Kate stared into the face of a huge guy she'd never set eyes on before.

'Kate Hardy. I want to see-'

'Mike Pendle. Yeah. We heard,' he said, raising a curious eyebrow. 'So did the rest of the bleedin' county. But he's upstairs.'

'Then let me up,' said Kate, taking a step forward.

'Can't do that love,' he said, blocking the whole doorway.

'Seriously. It's not the day to piss me off. Either let me in or get someone to fetch him. Now.'

The guy opened his mouth as if to argue, and then let out a huge sigh.

'Grey,' he called over his shoulder. 'Go tell his Highness that he's got a lady-caller gunning for his balls down here.'

If she wasn't so angry, that comment would have made her laugh. As it was, she just folded her arms protectively across her chest and tapped her foot.

'What the hell was that noise?' came a voice from inside. 'Stu?'

'He's all yours, love,' grinned the big guy, disappearing back inside and pointing Mike in her direction.

'Kate? This is a pleasant-'

'You *absolute* bastard,' she yelled, pushing forwards into the shop and poking him hard in the chest. She didn't care that there were half a dozen workmen she didn't know standing around them, staring at her like she had two heads. 'You could have seriously hurt us! You could have *killed* Stanley. You absolute, *absolute*-'

'Wow-wow-wow!' he said raising his hands in a small surrender motion and taking a couple of steps backwards. 'What are you going on about?'

'Don't pretend you don't know,' she spat. 'Stanley's still at the vet's. I've got to get Trixie fixed. I'm lucky I'm in one piece. And then I get back to The Sardine and you've complained to the f-' she paused briefly and took a breath in an attempt to stop her voice from going ultra-sonic and her language from descending further into the gutter.

'You complained to the council,' she said in a lower tone, 'about my outdoor tables.' She thrust the letter she was still clutching hard into his chest.

Mike flinched, grabbed the piece of paper and quickly scanned the letter from the council explaining that, following a complaint from members of Seabury's business community, it had come to their attention that Kate didn't hold the requisite licence to set up tables on the pavement outside The Sardine.

'I-' started Mike.

'No,' she said. 'No. You don't get to talk. I do. Play whatever stupid little games you want, but they won't work. You'll *never* kill off The Sardine. I've been here all my life - I'm not going anywhere. But if you *ever* do anything that puts me, my staff or my dog in danger again, then I will personally remove your balls and serve them to you for breakfast. Understood?'

Mike's mouth was hanging open, but he wasn't able to make any kind of sound. Good.

Kate snatched the letter back out of his hands, turned on her heel and, to the soundtrack of low whistles coming from the workmen, she stalked straight back outside.

Kate didn't slow her pace until she was back on the golden sand of West Beach. There was no way she was going to hang around near North Beach long enough for Mike Pendle to get over his shock and come up with some crummy excuse for his shitty behaviour. She'd just about managed not to take a swing at him back there, but she wasn't sure she'd manage it a second time.

Kicking off her shoes, Kate sank down into the sand and stared out at the sea. She just needed a moment to pull herself together before she headed back to The Sardine to face the inevitable questions from the others.

It felt so wrong to be down here on the beach without Stanley. She didn't know what she'd do if he was seriously hurt. What if she lost him? No, she couldn't even face that possibility.

Kate shook her head, trying to clear the bad thoughts as they crowded in on her. That wasn't going to happen. Stanley had a sore foot. She was just being dramatic. It was probably delayed shock from what had happened that morning - and that little scene back there.

She hated the fact that there was someone here in Seabury she now actively hated. She'd have to do her best to avoid bumping into him. Hell, in reality, that meant she'd have to avoid North Beach completely. This sucked!

Kate wiggled her toes in the sand then grabbed her mobile out of her pocket. It was time to act. She'd call the place they'd dropped Trixie off at earlier and find out if they'd had a chance to figure out how long the repairs would take.

Just as she pulled the details up on Google, the phone buzzed to life in her hands with an incoming call. It was the vet.

'Hello?' A cold drop of terror landed in her belly.

'Kate? We're all done with your boy.'

'Is he okay? Is it broken? Is there internal bleeding?' she gabbled.

'He's fine, Kate. It's a mild sprain. Nothing to be seen on the x-ray - better safe than sorry, though.'

'But all that yelping - are you sure he's okay?' she pressed, still not able to get the memory of Stanley's pathetic whimpering out of her head.

'Well, the poor boy had a massive blackthorn spike stuck in his paw!' said the vet. 'It was lodged right between his toes - that's why we missed it when we first looked him over. Very painful - but we got it out cleanly. They can turn really nasty, so I've given him a shot of antibiotics and I've given the area a good spray with antiseptic. You'll need to keep an eye on it for any swelling over the next few days, but it should be fine - it wasn't in there long.'

'So he's going to be okay?'

'He's absolutely fine. A couple of days taking it easy, and you won't even remember that it happened.'

Kate sighed. Chance would be a fine thing.

CHAPTER 10

Sunday. How was it Sunday already?! All Kate wanted to do was hide in bed all day watching romcoms and eating chocolate, but of course, she couldn't.

She knew that Sarah and Ethel would have both understood if she'd cancelled their plans for their get-together, but she just hadn't been able to bring herself to do it. If anything, they needed to re-group now more than ever.

After the initial shock of the accident had subsided a bit and Stanley was safely back in the flat - complete with extra treats and cuddles - it became apparent to Kate that Mike's move with the council was actually far more damaging than she'd first thought.

The letter demanded that she remove her external tables immediately and not replace them until she had applied for - and been granted - the proper licence. *If* she was granted the licence. This had halved her seating in one fell swoop.

Then, of course, she was still Trixie-less. The guys at the repair shop had said it would be about a week before they could fit the work in. That was a whole week without her delivery round... because, of course, she didn't actually *own* a car. What was the point when she never left Seabury?! It meant that she had to let her customers down yet again and, of course, it meant another cut in her takings. Quite a serious one.

So yes, today's meeting was far too important to cancel just because *she* needed a break. What The Sardine needed was some creative thinking, otherwise it would be in serious trouble before too long.

Kate knew that she needed to put on a brave face and a happy and enthusiastic front while the other two were here... but still, watching romcoms in her PJs really *was* very appealing right now.

She'd made one small concession to the fact that she was completely knackered, though. Instead of preparing an extravagant meal for the three of them as she had been planning to, she'd knocked up some pizza dough, whizzed up a batch of tomato sauce and gone to town with various toppings. Easy, delicious, and cooked in minutes rather than hours.

Kate hadn't actually seen Sarah since the day of the accident. The poor girl had been distraught about Stanley being hurt and had practically sobbed in relief when Kate had returned from the beach to share the good news that it wasn't serious.

Luckily, Charlie had still been there chatting away to the pair of them and had gladly offered her a lift to collect the invalid. Although Kate was super-grateful and accepted without hesitation, she suspected that this particular favour was designed to win him another of Ethel's much-coveted soft smiles above any thanks she could offer him.

By the time they'd returned, Ethel had sent Sarah home for the day, and Kate couldn't help but feel bad for all the drama. The poor girl hadn't been with them for long - what would she think?

The trilling of the doorbell combined with a booming bark from Stanley roused her from her thoughts, and she hurried downstairs.

'Ethel!' she said, forcing a smile onto her face. 'You're a bit early.'

'Hi! Yes - sorry about that. I just wanted a quick word before Sarah came up,'

'Why's that?' said Kate in surprise as she followed her friend up to the living room.

'Hello, my gorgeous boy!' crooned Ethel as Stanley mooched over for a tickle. 'How're you doing?'

'He's fine. His foot seems to be all better, other than a bit of a scab where that thorn was.'

'Not nice!' said Ethel with a tut. 'I still can't believe someone paid that vet bill for you, though!'

'That's Seabury for you,' said Kate, her smile instantly turning into a genuine one.

'True, true,' agreed Ethel. 'I wonder who it was. Probably one of your sandwich round customers, I reckon.'

Kate shrugged. She still couldn't believe it, no matter what she'd just said. She'd arrived to pick Stanley up, mildly dreading the hit her credit card was about to take and cursing the fact she hadn't taken out pet insurance, when the vet told her the bill had already been settled by a "concerned friend." When she'd asked who'd done such a lovely thing so that she could thank them, the vet had shaken her head and said she simply couldn't tell her - it was confidential.

'Well, whoever it was, I'm really grateful,' said Kate with a sigh. 'Not that I would begrudge emptying every account I have - as long as my boy's okay,' she added, earning herself a pat from Ethel. 'Anyway - I've learned my lesson. Stanley's now insured!'

'That's a very sensible idea,' said Ethel.

Just then the doorbell rang again.

'Bother. Kate - just quickly before you answer that - Sarah's got something she needs to talk to you about today.'

'O-kay,' said Kate, heading towards the stairs.

'Seriously - just - go easy on her, okay?'

'Easy...? Wait, what's going on?!'

'She needs to tell you herself. But - remember she's just a child, okay?'

Kate nodded. 'Of course. Is this what she wanted to tell me on Friday?'

Ethel nodded. 'Yes. But you've got to agree, that wasn't the moment.'

'Not the moment for anything, really,' said Kate with a wry smile.

The doorbell rang a second time and Kate bounded down the stairs to answer. She had to admit, she was curious. What on earth could lovely young Sarah have done to require such dire warnings from Ethel?

'Hiya!' said Sarah, her nervous smile wavering above yet another massive Tupperware box.

'Oooh... what have you been up to?' asked Kate, her eyes lighting up. 'More experimenting?'

'Yup,' said Sarah, nodding. 'I had an idea for The Sardine. Actually - a couple of ideas. But I need to speak to you about something first.'

'No probs,' said Kate, keeping her tone deliberately light. 'Come on up and we'll get a drink.'

'How's Stanley?' asked Sarah, puffing up the stairs behind her.

'Almost fully mended.'

'Thank God,' breathed Sarah.

'He'll be glad to see you! He doesn't think much of walkies being suspended,' laughed Kate. That was an understatement. Stanley had been going stir-crazy. The vet had advised her just to give him very short walks for a couple of days, and she'd been keeping him off the beaches - North Beach so that he wasn't scrambling over stones making his sprain worse, and West Beach so that he didn't get sand in the puncture left behind by the thorn.

Kate had been right. The minute Sarah stepped into the living room - before she'd even had the chance to put her box down - the big bear was there at her feet, leaning his weight against her legs and staring lovingly up at her.

'Here, let me take that so you two can hug it out,' laughed Kate, taking the Tupperware from Sarah's arms.

Sarah dropped down next to Stanley and wrapped her arms around him, and he leant his huge head on her shoulder.

Kate watched them for a moment. That's what Stanley always did to her when she was worried about something. Hm. Ethel was right. She needed to be gentle with Sarah - no matter what the girl was about to tell her, she was worried enough about it that Stanley had already picked up on something.

'Tea Sarah?' called Ethel from the kitchen.

'Please!' she called back, her voice muffled through a layer of hairy dog.

'Did you have a good day off yesterday?' asked Kate, perching on the sofa. She was hoping this little opener might ease the way into the conversation.

Sarah shrugged. 'I'd have preferred to be at The Sardine!'

'Well... sadly the law says that I can't use you as slave labour!' laughed Kate.

Sarah smiled back at her.

'So - when I came back from all that chaos on Friday, you wanted to talk to me about something? Sorry I stormed out before we got the chance!'

Kate watched the colour leach out of Sarah's face, and mentally kicked herself. Maybe the blunt approach wasn't the best one. Still, she wanted to make the most out of this evening, and there was no way she was going to be able to do that while they were dancing around whatever this big revelation was.

Kate watched as Stanley scooted his bum around so he was practically sitting on Sarah, and the girl couldn't help but let out a small laugh as he nearly knocked her over.

'Okay boy, I'm okay,' she said.

'You want to tell me?' asked Kate gently.

Sarah looked at her directly. 'I wish I had told you straight away. But... well, I really wanted the chance to work for you. And I love it so much. But after everything that's happened... is happening... you need to know. But I...'

Sarah paused and Kate watched her closely. She didn't have a clue what the girl was about to confide in her, but it was certainly costing her a lot to get it out.

'Look - I'll get it if you don't want me to work for you anymore,' she said, her voice sounding shaky.

'It's not going to come to that, lass.' Ethel's voice in

the doorway made Kate jump slightly. She'd been so focused on the scared girl in front of her, she'd briefly forgotten that her old friend was there too.

'Okay,' sighed Sarah. 'Well, you wanted to know about my parents.'

Kate raised her eyebrows in surprise, but kept her mouth shut.

'I live with my dad now. My mum's with a... a... well, she's with this other guy. She's divorcing my dad, and it's... it's really bad for him.' Sarah paused and swallowed.

'I'm really sorry, Sarah,' said Kate. 'I get it. I don't know if Ethel told you, but I lived with my dad too. A bit different because I lost my own mum, but I know how hard this stuff can be.'

Sarah nodded. 'It's not just that though.'

'Oh?'

'God, you're going to hate me,' she said, earning herself a wet nose in the cheek from Stanley.

'I can promise you, there's no way that's possible,' said Kate gently, wondering what awful story this poor girl was carrying around with her.

'Okay, but I get it if you do,' she paused and took a deep breath. 'My dad's Mike Pendle.'

Kate froze. Sarah was Mike Pendle's daughter? As in - second-generation New York Froth? The guy who had attacked her business and run her and Stanley off the road?

'See. I told you you'd hate me,' said Sarah, her chin trembling with emotion.

Kate swiftly shook her head. 'I don't. Not at all. It's just a - surprise.' She paused and swallowed, trying to gather her thoughts. 'Can I ask you a question?'

'Course,' said Sarah in a small voice.

'What does he think about you working for me. Was it his idea?'

Sarah shook her head in surprise. 'Definitely not - he doesn't even know!'

'He doesn't *know*?!' echoed Kate. 'But you've been in The Sardine for hours every day - how'd you swing that?'

Sarah shrugged. 'He's been really busy trying to get the flat sorted for us and... the café,' she added awkwardly. 'He hasn't had time to notice much else, I guess.'

Kate blinked a couple of times, and then her behaviour on Friday came back to her in full force. The tirade she'd gone on. The things she'd said about Sarah's *dad*! If she'd have known, she would never, ever have said anything in front of the girl.

'Oh Sarah, I'm so, so sorry!' said Kate seriously.

'*You're* sorry? What for?!'

'For everything I said on Friday. About your dad!'

Sarah shrugged. 'You didn't know. And anyway, if he *did* those things - going to the council, I mean - then he's been well out of order.'

Kate frowned.

'But there's no way that was dad in the car - you know - with the accident.'

Kate shook her head. That had been Mike Pendle's car and no mistake. But it wasn't fair to discuss it with Sarah. Not at all. It hadn't been her driving, had it? It wasn't as though Sarah had any control over her dad's behaviour.

'Look. That's between me and your dad,' said Kate quietly. 'I'm really sorry you got caught in the middle.'

'It's my fault for not telling you,' muttered Sarah.

'Okay - well, you've told me now. The question is, do you want to carry on at The Sardine? Because I'd love you to stay.'

Sarah stared at her, wide-eyed. 'Seriously?'

'Seriously!' laughed Kate.

Sarah nodded. 'I really, really do.'

'Well, that's settled then. But there *is* one condition.'

'Anything,' said Sarah eagerly.

'You have to tell your dad you're working with me.'

'Aw, really?' sighed Sarah. 'He'll go totally mental.'

'He's going to find out sooner or later anyway,' said Ethel gently. 'That's just the way things are around here.'

'Ethel's right. It's a miracle he hasn't already found out. Better coming from you than someone like Veronica.'

Sarah nodded. 'Okay.'

'I can talk to him about it if you need me to,' said Kate. It really cost her to say that. Every ounce of her being wanted to keep as much distance between her and Mike bloody Pendle as possible. But she owed it to Sarah to make this as easy as she could.

'Really?' said Sarah, surprise on her face. 'You'd do that?'

Kate nodded firmly. 'If it means we get to keep working together, then yes - I'll answer any questions he's got for me.'

'Thank you,' said Sarah, grinning at her, relief flooding her face. 'You're amazing.'

'You're not so bad yourself, you know,' laughed Kate.

CHAPTER 11

'Well then,' said Ethel from the doorway, brushing a tear from her eye. 'If you two have quite finished?'

Kate laughed and threw a cushion at Ethel, who caught it deftly.

'Right!' said Sarah, pulling herself together and nodding at Ethel. 'Kate – we've got something to show you.'

'You have?'

They both nodded. Sarah scrambled up from the floor and made her way over to the doorway - Stanley glued to her side. The three of them then stood staring at Kate with identical grins on their faces.

'Come on,' said Ethel, 'we need to go outside.'

'Don't you want to make the pizzas?' said Kate, getting to her feet.

'This won't take long. And trust me – you're going to want to see it.'

The four of them made a procession down the stairs, led by Sarah with Ethel bringing up the rear.

'Where are we going?' said Kate as they spilled out of the side door.

'Follow me!' said Ethel.

She led them around to the front of the café. Kate paused, half expecting them to be going into The Sardine.

'You know, we should have blindfolded her,' muttered Sarah.

'Ha – she'd never have agreed,' said Ethel.

'I might have!' said Kate with a snort.

'Well, too late now!' said Sarah, coming to a stop in front of Trixie's yard and pointing.

Kate's heart leapt. Somehow, she half expected to find that the pair of them had managed to work a miracle and get Trixie fixed early - but it wasn't that. She was dumbfounded by the sight that met her eyes.

Trixie was still nowhere to be seen, but neither was her grubby, unloved little yard.

'What on earth…?' murmured Kate, taking a couple of steps forwards before stopping again and bringing her hand to her mouth.

The wrought-iron gate stood wide open and the dim, slightly dank yard had been transformed into something straight out of a fairy tale. There was a gaggle of small tables - complete with a couple of chairs apiece - all set with blue and white striped linen tablecloths. The old stone walls around the sides looked like they had been swept, and now glittered with an array of tiny lights that had been strung across their rough surfaces.

All the random tat she usually stored in the yard along with Trixie had miraculously disappeared, and the cobbles had been weeded and swept. There was even an old barrel over in the corner that looked like it had been turned into a makeshift station for cutlery and condiments.

'This is just to give you an idea of what it could be like,' said Sarah, sounding excited. 'We had to do it quite quickly - we didn't want you turning up and ruining the surprise - but of course, there could be loads more decorations, and proper place settings and everything.'

'You two... you two did all this on your own?' asked Kate, unable to tear her eyes from the scene.

'Well no - Charlie helped,' said Ethel with a smile.

'He's a keeper, that one!' said Kate.

'Well, he's not mine to keep,' said Ethel quickly. 'Anyway - what do you think?' she pressed, gesturing at the yard.

'I love it. It would never have crossed my mind to use it like this!' she said, wandering forwards and running her hand across the back of one of the chairs. 'I mean, *how* have I never thought to use it like this? It's perfect. It's beautiful... and doesn't it look like it's already been part of the café for years?!' she laughed.

Kate couldn't believe this. There was more than enough room to navigate between the tables comfortably, and the view out through the gate, right down across the beach to the sea was magical.

'Well,' said Sarah, 'we were trying to figure out what we could do about space for more customers until you get the outdoor tables sorted out, and this idea came up. Without Trixie in here, we thought it was the perfect time to give it a go.'

'All the tables and chairs fold up, so you can still move them out of the way to lock Trixie in overnight,' said Ethel.

Kate nodded. 'Erm, where did you get them?'

'Borrowed them from the town hall,' said Ethel. 'They don't mind - they're hardly ever used!'

'Plus,' said Sarah, 'like we were talking about before, Trixie's trailer is sign-painted for The Sardine - so she's like an advertisement on wheels. It makes more sense for her to be parked up somewhere where visitors can spot her - at least during the day when you're not using her.'

Kate nodded again. A strange tingling sensation seemed to be travelling down her arms. Excitement? Fear of all this change? She wasn't sure which!

'Of course, if you don't like it, it's not the end of the world,' said Ethel, quietly moving closer and linking arms with her. 'All it means is that this place has had a much-needed tidy-up!' she chuckled.

'No - I *adore* it,' said Kate, staring around her. She pulled out one of the chairs, sat down and watched Stanley as he snuffled around the edges of the newly cleaned yard.

It *should* feel cramped, dark and unappealing in here, but it was quite the opposite. You could smell the salty sea air, but the walls provided shelter from the breeze and the blazing sunshine alike. It felt cosy and cute, and... pretty much perfect.

'We could add a few little decorative touches here and there like Sarah suggested,' said Kate thoughtfully, 'some leafy plants hanging here and there on the walls and in those little alcoves?'

Sarah nodded, looking around. 'That'd look brilliant - and maybe bring in a couple of seaside themed bits too?'

'Nice!' said Kate, then shook her head in disbelief. 'You realise this has more than doubled the seating we already had?'

Ethel nodded, plonking herself down in the chair next to Kate. 'That's not the best bit, though.'

'It's not?!' laughed Kate.

'Well no. We were thinking you could get one of the local sailmakers to rig something up overhead. It would give you even more shade when the sun's high as well as shelter if it rains. Then in the autumn and maybe some of the winter, you could pop one of those outdoor space heaters out here.'

'And if it's a sail instead of a proper roof, you could still roll it up and pack it away like you do with the awning when there's going to be high winds or whatever,' said Sarah

'You two've thought of everything!' grinned Kate.

'You ain't heard nothing yet!' said Sarah, excitedly.

'Well... no,' said Ethel. 'But how about we go get that ice cream you promised us before we carry on?'

'Ethel Watts!' laughed Kate, 'pudding before the main course? You rebel!'

Ethel grinned, looking more than a bit naughty. 'All this excitement has got me feeling... adventurous!'

'So, here's a question for you both,' said Kate, taking a massive lick of Black Forest Gateau ice cream as they wandered, three-abreast with Stanley ambling along ahead of them, back towards West Beach. 'Do you think it would be worth opening the café on Sundays?'

'Nope,' chorused the other two at exactly the same time.

Kate spluttered out a laugh. 'Jeez, don't hold back!'

Sarah shrugged. 'How many customers did you just see in Nana's?'

'Well - three,' said Kate, 'if you count us.'

'And how many people do you see pottering around

right now?' said Ethel, waving her mint choc-chip cone at the deserted seafront.

'Just us,' sighed Kate. 'Oh wait - there's Lionel down there.'

'He's painting,' laughed Sarah, staring down towards the sea where Lionel had set up his easel. 'He doesn't exactly count as a potential customer.'

'I bet you he'd be in at some point in the day if we opened on Sundays.'

'Well, yes,' said Ethel again, 'but he might well be the only one. We just don't get the visitors in town on Sundays. Not that we get that many any day of the week. I've never understood why Frank opens Nana's for the entire afternoon and evening on a Sunday, other than to make new stock!'

'Dad never opened any of the cafes on a Sunday,' said Sarah, shrugging. 'Don't think he's planning on doing it here either. He always said the cost of staffing was more than the takings - and that everyone should have one day where there's no chance of getting called into work for some emergency or other.' She paused, and suddenly look freaked out. 'Sorry, I shouldn't talk about him.'

Kate glanced at Sarah and shook her head. 'Don't apologise - that's actually really good advice. I *do* forget about things like having a life - The Sardine *is* my life. But you're totally right - it's good to have a day I can tell Pierre that I definitely won't be working.'

'Pfft,' said Ethel. 'Not sure *he's* a good enough reason, to be honest.'

'Oi!' laughed Kate. 'I'm happy, okay?'

'Are you really?' asked Ethel.

'Erm - is Stanley allowed down onto the beach?' asked Sarah sounding awkward. She grabbed hold of Stanley's collar just in time to stop him from launching down onto the sand.

'Here!' said Kate, taking his lead from her pocket and tossing it to Sarah. 'We'll keep him on that to slow him up a bit - but I reckon he'll be okay! A bit of saltwater would probably be quite good for his foot to be honest.'

Kate and Ethel watched as Sarah clipped the lead to Stanley's collar and then head down onto the sand with him.

'Anyway,' said Kate in a low voice now that Sarah was briefly out of earshot, 'bit rich you having a go about Pierre when you're pining for a certain Mr Endicott, isn't it?!'

'Pining?!' grunted Ethel. 'I'm hardly pining. He's in the café most days.'

'Yes, and we all know why that is,' retorted Kate.

Ethel nodded, a mulish expression on her usually serene face. 'Because he's delivering your veg - and because he's now addicted to your coffee.'

'Oh, give over,' laughed Kate. 'The man's head over heels in love with you... and I'm starting to wonder if you might actually feel the same way?!'

'What would make you say that?' said Ethel, pushing past her and climbing down onto the beach.

'Oh nothing, just that you go bright pink any time anyone mentions him, and when you see him, or when you're talking about him,' said Kate following her friend down onto the sand. She kept her voice light and playful, but there was no chance Ethel was going to fob her off so easily this time.

Ethel glanced down the beach towards Sarah and Stanley who were pottering together along the tideline, Sarah now carrying her sandals so that she could paddle with Stanley. Then she turned back to Kate.

'So what if I *do* have feelings for him?' she practically growled, looking decidedly uncomfortable all of a sudden. 'There's nothing to be done.'

'There's *everything* to be done!' said Kate looking thrilled.

'No,' said Ethel decidedly, 'there isn't. I'm too old for any of that nonsense. And besides...'

'What?' prodded Kate gently. 'Besides, *what?*'

'He has never *once* told me that he feels anything for me. At all. It's probably just all in my head.'

'I promise you it isn't,' said Kate carefully.

'Well - even if it isn't, there is *no way* I'm doing or saying *anything* - understand? It's up to him to make the first move - not that he ever will. But until that happens, can we just *drop it?!*'

Kate could see that the usually serene Ethel was getting more than a little worked up and felt bad. It hadn't been her intention to upset her friend - only to encourage her. After all, if two people loved each other, like these two clearly did (at least - it was clear to the entire town, even if it wasn't to them) then surely they should be together? *Deserved* to be together. Life was far too short to miss out on things like true love.

'Can I just say one more thing, then I promise I'll shut up?'

Ethel gave a curt nod.

'Charlie isn't really the kind of man who tells you what he's thinking or how he feels, is he? He's the kind of man who shows you.'

'And how has he shown me?' said Ethel, raising an eyebrow.

'Well... answer me this. Has he ever come into the café without bringing you a gift of some kind?' she asked. 'And the other day when he rescued me and Stanley doesn't count!' she added quickly.

'He...' Ethel paused, her eyes seeming to unfocus as she thought about it. 'I...'

'Exactly,' said Kate.

Ethel frowned and then shook her head. 'Come on, let's go and join those two for a paddle - we've still got loads of ideas to talk about, and today was meant to be about The Sardine, not our love lives!'

Kate chuckled. 'Okay, you're on,' she said, linking her arm through Ethel's as they strode down the beach towards the sea.

CHAPTER 12

Kate cursed. The knock on the flat door made her jump so much that the pages she'd been carefully setting out on her coffee table fluttered to the floor.

'Balls,' she muttered again, hastily gathering them back together and dumping them in a heap onto the table. She'd just managed to get them in some kind of order too.

Kate wondered who it could be. In theory, no one other than Sarah and Ethel knew that she was hiding out up in her flat. They'd agreed that while Trixie was off the road, Kate would cancel her sandwich round rather than trying to borrow a car and use the time to do some much-needed planning while Ethel and Sarah manned the café. Most of the businesses she delivered to had agreed to pick up orders directly from The

Sardine as it was only a short-term break - which was a huge relief.

Kate was busy delving deeper into the ideas they'd all brainstormed the other night - and she had to admit, she'd spent quite a lot of time quivering with both fear and excitement. Of course, they wouldn't be able to run with everything, but the possibilities seemed endless. Cake baking and simple cookery workshops, cute hen-do evenings in the yard, afternoon teas delivered on Trixie, weddings, cake subscription boxes... "a taste of the seaside"... the ideas were bonkers and wonderful.

Now Kate was busy gathering quotes, crunching the numbers and doing some market research to see what had legs. One thing was for sure, the little yard was already a huge hit with customers, and her visitor numbers were already going up.

Whoever was at the flat door thumped again and the sound was met by an echoing bark from Stanley who'd been snoozing in his bed.

'Stay there, lad,' she said.

Another knock sounded and she tutted.

'Alright, I'm coming, I'm coming!' she yelled,

Kate hurtled down the stairs hoping there wasn't some kind of emergency in the café - though surely they'd have just called her mobile? Flinging the door open, she stopped dead. There, in front of her, was the last person she'd expected to find on her doorstep.

'I think we need to talk,' said Mike Pendle.

'O-kay...' said Kate. Ah. Of course. Sarah must have finally spoken to him about her job at The Sardine. She should have been expecting this really. She was just about to take a step backwards to let him in, then abruptly changed her mind. 'What about?' she asked. She didn't want to assume this was about Sarah, only to find out it was something else.

'Sarah,' he said, raising his hands in the kind of gesture that said "*duh, what else?*"

Kate nodded. 'Okay, shall we go to the café?'

Mike shook his head. 'Maybe somewhere a bit more private?' he said, his face deadly serious. 'Somewhere Sarah can't hear us, I mean.'

'Well, I *would* invite you up,' said Kate, 'but Stanley's up there.'

Mike swallowed. 'Okay, how about a stroll on the beach?'

Kate shrugged. It was definitely better than having to invite her least favourite person up to her little sanctuary. 'Sure.'

'So,' said Kate as she pulled the door carefully closed behind her, 'I'm guessing Sarah has told you that she's been working for me?'

Mike nodded and glanced at her as they crossed the little road and headed down onto the sand. 'She has. I have to say, I'm quite surprised that you haven't been in touch before now - just as a courtesy.'

Uh oh. So this was going to be one of *those* kinds of conversations, was it?

Suddenly she was very glad that they were outside on the beach, with the soft breeze blowing through her hair and plenty of space around them, rather than trapped together in her flat.

'Well, to be honest, I would have spoken to you as soon as she started, but Sarah didn't actually tell me she was related to you until Sunday.'

'Ah, right. That explains a lot.' Mike sighed and frowned at the sea.

He looked quite bizarre down here in the fresh air. With a crisp white shirt and suit jacket over dark chinos and silly, pointy dress shoes, he stood out like a sore thumb. Kate briefly struggled to contain a smile. He really did have a lot to learn about living in Seabury.

'Look,' she said, 'don't be too hard on her. I think she just felt really awkward and didn't want it to affect her chances of getting the job.'

Mike nodded, frowning, but didn't say anything.

'She's a great worker - makes a mean cup of coffee, the customers love her, she's bursting with ideas and her baking is incredible!'

'Of course she's a great worker,' Mike snapped. 'Sorry. What I mean to say is that she's been in and out of cafes all her life - and she's been working in New York Froth at weekends for ages.'

'That explains why she's such a natural, then.'

Mike nodded. 'She told to me that she wanted to

work with you because of learning more about the baking side of things. From Edna?'

'Ethel,' corrected Kate. 'She's a genius - it's a great opportunity for Sarah. It sounds like she really knows what she wants to do.'

'But she doesn't. She's just a kid!'

'Which makes it even more impressive!' exclaimed Kate. 'Just imagine how far she could take it if she follows her dream now.'

'There'll be plenty of time for all that after A-levels and university. I don't want her wasting her brain, and I don't want her working in a café when she could be studying.'

'Unless it's your café!' muttered Kate.

'That's different. You just want her because she comes pre-trained,' he spat. 'And what a *great* chance for you to pick her brains about my business.'

'You really do think a lot of yourself, don't you?' said Kate, incredulously. 'Of *course* it's a massive bonus that Sarah knows what she's doing and knows how to deal with customers - but I hired her before I knew she had anything to do with you.'

'But *now* you know, it's got to stop.'

'No, don't say that!' She took a deep breath, trying to stay calm. 'Look, Sarah seems to be happy at The Sardine - surely that's important to you?'

'Of course it bloody well is,' said Mike, raking his hand through his hair.

'Well then - let her stay. She's getting to know the

locals and finding her place here! I'd never dream of getting in her way if - when you've opened up New York Froth - she wants to come back to work for you...'

Mike let out a bitter laugh. 'But she won't. It's all about the bloody baking for her.'

'Then I promise she'll learn loads with us, but I'd never put her in a position where I ask about your business, okay? For the moment, we've said it's just for the summer holidays - until she knows whether she's going back to school or on to college in September. I said we'd talk things through again then.'

'She'll be going back to school,' he said, his voice flat and determined. 'But if it's just for the summer then... fine, I guess it's okay.' Mike scuffed his shoe through the sand. 'How's Stanley now?'

Kate's spine stiffened. 'Mending.'

'Thank goodness,' said Mike.

She tried to bite down the retort - for Sarah's sake, more than anything - but there was no stopping it. 'Like you care,' she muttered.

'*Excuse* me?! Look, Sarah told me about your accident. Actually, she yelled at me for it.'

'Can you blame her?'

'If I really had done what you think I did, then no - I wouldn't blame her - *or* you! But I didn't.'

'It was your car!'

'It *was* my car. My ex-wife came to pick it up from me - she got it in the divorce. I was just using it to get Sarah's stuff moved down here. If it really *was* my car that caused that accident - then it was *her* driving that day.'

Kate opened her mouth to retort, then closed it again. Was he telling the truth? She jumped as his hand shot out and gently caught hold of her arm, pulling her around to face him. 'You *have* to believe me. I would never, ever have done that.'

Kate stared at him feeling like her world had just tilted somehow. 'Well then,' she blustered, trying to wrap her head around this, 'tell your wife-'

'Ex-wife!'

'Yeah, her. You can tell her she's not welcome back here. And it's not a good idea for her to come anywhere near me.'

Mike raised an eyebrow. 'Well, no. After witnessing your protective streak first-hand, I can see she'd have quite a lot to worry about.'

'Then tell her to stay away,' growled Kate.

'Nah,' said Mike, and for the very first time, Kate saw a tiny smile pull at the corner of his mouth, his eyes taking on a mischievous look. 'I'd actually pay good money to see you take her down.' He cleared his throat. 'For what it's worth, I'm *really* sorry that happened to you and Stanley and... Trixie?'

Kate raised an eyebrow. The fact he'd just called Trixie by her name rather than "that heap of rust" made her realise that he was trying to make an effort. Damn. It was much easier when she could just straight-out hate him.

'Well, I guess I owe you an apology,' she muttered, 'for yelling at you - especially in front of your staff.'

'Nah. The guys thought it was hilarious.'

'Oh.' Kate scratched her nose. 'Who were those guys anyway?'

'Why? Want to poach them to do some work on your place?'

'You don't give up do you?' she said, incredulously. 'For one thing, no, and for another, if I wanted work done on my place, I'd hire local builders from here in Seabury. You'll have put an awful lot of noses out of joint by bringing them in when we've got great guys here in town who *need* the work.'

Mike shrugged. 'That's business.'

'It's not how business is done in Seabury. We support our own. We try to keep cash *within* our community. It's how it works.'

'Well, these guys are from Plymouth. They're about half the price and hiring them means I can open up much sooner and give you a run for your money.'

Kate let out an exasperated sound.

'What?!' he demanded.

'Nothing. I need to get back.'

'Oh yeah - Sarah mentioned - you've gotta work out a plan now the council's causing you problems, I guess?'

'I... you...' spluttered Kate.

'What?'

'Nothing. But if you *ever* need someone to tell you

how things *really* work around here - you know, when you decide that you actually want to fit in rather than alienating everyone around you and getting the council to do your dirty work - *do* come and visit!'

'You know, you really need to get your facts straight!' said Mike, his eyes flashing.

'Are you or are you not employing a bunch of people to work on fitting up your café who have to drive in from Plymouth every day?'

'I am, but-'

'Instead of the local guys?'

'Yes and I already told you why - but-'

'Then I rest my case,' said Kate.

'Look. If you want The Sardine to survive, you need to open your eyes and accept reality!' he said, starting to raise his voice in agitation.

'And you need to stop being a... a...'

'A what?' he demanded.

'A grumpy badger!' she spat, turning on her heel and marching across the sand, putting as much distance between them as quickly as she could.

CHAPTER 13

'What happened, what happened, what happened?' chanted Sarah the minute Kate walked into the café.

Kate slumped into one of the chairs and Sarah followed suit in the one opposite her.

'Give her a second, girl!' said Ethel, tutting at her from the kitchen, and watching Kate in concern as she rested her head in her hands. 'Okay - that's a long enough second, Kate. What happened!'

Kate quickly looked around her. 'No customers?'

'Plenty,' laughed Ethel, 'but they're all out in the yard. 'Come on, quick. I've got a round of teacakes toasting.'

'Well,' said Kate, 'I'm guessing you know Mike - your dad, I mean - came up to see me.'

'Course we do,' nodded Sarah, 'we told him where you were!'

'Yeah - thanks so much for that!' muttered Kate.

'*Annnnnnd?*' demanded Sarah. 'Do I still have a job? What happened?'

'Well - I, erm, I just called your dad a… a… grumpy badger,' said Kate, wincing and burying her face in her hands.

Sarah let out a massive snort and Ethel started chuckling from behind the counter.

'Guys! It's not funny!!'

'Are you kidding? That's frickin' hilarious. Oooh, I'm never going to let him live that one down. It's going in every single birthday card, every-'

'Don't you dare, or you're sacked,' said Kate, glaring at Sarah.

Sarah, however, didn't even flinch. 'So, does that mean I've still got a job to be sacked from, then?' she asked.

Kate nodded. 'Yes. For the summer. As long as you don't tell me anything about his business!'

'Like I would anyway. Well, that's better than nothing,' said Sarah with a grin.

'Yep - he said you'll be going back to school in September…'

Sarah's smile dropped.

'Don't look like that. It gives us plenty of time to figure out a plan to convince him college is right for you - if that's what you want.'

'You'd help me do that?'

'Course we will,' said Ethel, 'on one condition.'

'Which is?'

'Take this lot out to table six for me!' she said pointing at a tray laden with buttery teacakes.

'You've got it!' said Sarah, leaping to her feet, grabbing the tray and heading straight outside.

'So, how'd it really go? From what you just told Sarah, that's a great outcome, so why the dramatics?' asked Ethel.

'Mike just told me it was his ex-wife who ran me and Stanley off the road,' she muttered. 'Not him.'

'Oh.'

'You already knew, didn't you?' said Kate, staring at her.

'Sarah told me this morning.'

'And you didn't think to warn me?'

'It was a bit late by then, love. Mike was already at your door!'

'I'm so embarrassed. I went absolutely ape-sh-... bananas at him the other day!'

Ethel bit her lip, clearly trying to stop herself from laughing. 'I know. But I'm sure he understood? I mean, you didn't know at that point if Stanley was going to be okay, did you? And you were in shock yourself.'

Kate nodded, cupping her face in her hands. 'He understood. And he did apologise for what his ex did - even though it had nothing to do with him other than happening in his old car. I mean, he brought the subject up to start with - asked how Stanley was - and he doesn't even like dogs!'

'Who?' said Sarah, bouncing back through the door. 'My dad?'

Ethel nodded at her.

'Yeah, well - there's a reason for that. He'd hate me telling you though.'

'Better not, then,' said Kate, though she was definitely intrigued.

Sarah shrugged. 'Okay. It's pretty nasty, actually.'

Ethel raised her eyebrows at Kate, who subtly shook her head. She was going to start as she meant to go on - she was *never* going to put Sarah in the position where she felt like she was snitching on her dad.

'Oh,' said Sarah, 'one thing I did find out that I think you should know - and then I promise we'll go back to pretending that I don't even know him - he's the one who paid Stanley's vet bill.'

'He *what?!*' said Ethel and Kate at the same time.

'Yup. Sounds like he was so worried after you'd been to see him that day, he called to find out if Stanley was going to be okay and paid for the x-ray and everything.'

'But why?!' said Kate. 'He didn't even know that... that... erm...'

'That my bitch of a mother was responsible?' said Sarah. 'He'll have put two and two together.'

Kate flinched and she saw Ethel nearly drop the teacup she was holding. It was the first time Sarah had ever mentioned her mum. She looked at the girl's face, trying to judge whether this was something they needed to talk about or brush straight past for now.

'It's okay,' said Sarah. 'I know what she's like. Always have. She's a nasty piece of work and I've had to put up with her for years. She only had me because dad wanted kids. *She* told me that. When I was about six. That's why I'm so happy dad's finally away from her and I get to live with him!'

'Oh. Okay,' said Kate, thrown by the matter-of-fact way the girl had just delivered these heart-breaking titbits. *Poor Sarah!*

'Look, dad's been through the shittiest of shit times,' said Sarah in a low voice. 'I *know* he can be a bit of a prat. He's like captain awkward when it comes to change, and making friends, and talking to new people. But underneath everything, he's actually really kind. A good guy.'

Sarah paused and Kate watched her try to regain full control of her feelings a moment.

'Though,' said Sarah, raising an eyebrow as a smirk appeared on her face, 'I think Grumpy Badger is still going to be his name from now until the day he dies!'

Spotting an elderly couple in the doorway, Sarah quickly plastered a professional smile on her face. 'Good morning! We've got seats in here or there are still tables available out in our gorgeous courtyard if you'd prefer?'

This transition to smooth waitress-mode almost made Kate laugh out loud.

'Ooh, courtyard please!' said the elderly woman, beaming at Sarah.

'Of course, let me take you to a table and we'll bring your order out to you.'

Sarah led them back outside and Kate turned, open-mouthed to Ethel who was standing in the kitchen with her hand over her heart.

'Well I never!' said the older woman. 'He paid for Stanley!'

'Right?' said Kate. 'Now I feel even worse!'

'Nothing that can't be solved by a proper, calm apology at some point, love,' said Ethel. 'But I have to ask, what's with the Grumpy Badger bit?'

'He was being a prat about business stuff, and the issues with the council - which *he* caused - and about using that company from Plymouth instead of the guys from Seabury! And I just lost it and told him that when he wanted to find out how things worked around here, he should come to me, as long as he'd stopped being-'

'A grumpy badger?' snorted Ethel.

'Precisely.'

Sarah's bombshell had completely derailed Kate's day, so when Charlie turned up with several extra crates laden with soft fruit, it took her a moment or two to figure out what was going on.

'Yer order, Kate! I have to say, I'm *that* excited about

the idea of being able to get a box of cakes every week. And everyone up at the allotments loves the idea of your cream tea packs too!'

Kate shook her head and forced herself back to life. The cake boxes - of course! That's why she'd ordered so much fruit! She, Ethel and Sarah had decided to trial the cake subscription boxes locally - as well as another gem of an idea - cream tea in a box. Scones, jam, cream and some fancy-pants, individually wrapped teabags. Ethel had promptly declared that she'd better get more jam made, so Kate had asked Charlie to help her out.

'Couldn't grab a cuppa and a cheese toastie while I'm here, could I?' he asked.

'Of course,' said Ethel.

'Thanks. Tis hot work picking these blighters,' he said, pointing at the plump gooseberries.

'Just you wait until I've had my way with them,' she beamed, 'I'll save a jar for you.'

'Much obliged,' he murmured turning pink. 'Oh. Wait a sec - I'll be right back.'

He scuttled back out of the café and Kate, who'd started ferrying the crates of fruit into the tiny, cool store cupboard at the back of the café to keep them fresh for later, raised her eyebrows. 'What was all that about?'

'No idea,' said Ethel, starting to grate fresh cheese for a toastie with a little smile on her face.

'*I* know!' said Sarah, nodding at the door.

The other two turned just in time to see Charlie reappear with a huge bunch of flowers in his arms.

'I brought these for you, Ethel, from the allotments.'

'For me?'

Charlie nodded.

Ethel dumped the block of cheese back onto the chopping board and hurried around the counter towards him.

Kate paused in the kitchen, not wanting to interrupt by going over to fetch the last crate of fruit.

'I thought you might like 'em?' said Charlie, thrusting the flowers into Ethel's arms.

'They're beautiful!' she breathed, inspecting the different blooms.

'Tha's larkspur, and that deep purple is-'

'Dahlia!' she said with a sigh of happiness. 'My-'

'Favourite,' said Charlie, nodding. 'And then those white ones are campanula.'

'Oh Charlie, they're gorgeous, thank you!'

'Tis my pleasure. Picked 'em messell.'

Kate jumped as Sarah squeeze her hand in excitement. The two of them were now standing, watching the little scene unfold in rapt silence.

'So - what was it you wanted to drink with your toastie?' asked Ethel lightly, unable to take her eyes off the flowers, but clearly making a valiant attempt to get back onto more familiar ground.

'Tea please.'

'Tea?'

Charlie nodded. 'Tea. I'll take a pot if you care to share one?'

'I... well... we're quite busy...' she said, flustered, turning to Kate as if looking for help.

'You're due a break!' said Kate.

Ethel glared at her. Clearly that wasn't the response she'd been looking for.

'I'll finish off Charlie's toastie and bring it out to you, if you'd like to sit outside?' said Sarah, a mischievous grin on her face.

'Tha's right kind of you,' said Charlie, smiling at her.

'I'll get these in some water and be out in a mo,' said Ethel, ushering Charlie back out of the café. As soon as he was out of sight she turned to the pair of them in the kitchen. 'Interfering wenches,' she spluttered, making them both laugh.

'I'll take those,' said Kate, grabbing the flowers from her friend. 'I'll pop them in some water and stand them out with the fruit to keep them cool.'

Ethel was still glaring back and forth between the two of them.

'Why are you still here?' laughed Sarah. 'Your date's waiting!'

'I... I...' Ethel cleared her throat. 'He knew my favourite flower,' she finally managed to say.

'I know - how cute!' said Sarah, not looking at her as she carefully moved Charlie's toastie onto the grill.

'I'm nervous,' said Ethel in a quiet voice.

Kate stared at her, open-mouthed. 'Why? It's just Charlie. You've known him forever.'

'But... he knew my favourite flower,' she said again, wonder in her voice, as if she was confirming the fact to herself rather than speaking to Kate. 'This changes *everything!*'

'It's a cup of tea with a friend,' said Kate stoutly, watching Ethel carefully now. She'd never seen her like this before, and Kate wondered if Ethel was considering making a dash for her cottage instead of joining Charlie outside. 'Just a cup of tea with lovely Charlie,' she repeated.

'Right. You're right,' said Ethel, giving herself a little shake. 'I won't be long.'

'Take as long as you need. Oh - and invite him to the party while you're out there? I forgot earlier!' said Kate.

They both watched her march out of The Sardine and turn towards the yard, and then Kate turned to look at Sarah.

'Well!' said Kate.

'I *know!*' said Sarah with a huge smile on her face. 'Charlie's about to get *so* lucky!'

CHAPTER 14

The rest of the week disappeared in a haze of preparations for the party. It had been Sarah's idea to get a bunch of their regulars together one evening, make use of their gorgeous new courtyard, and have a tasting session for their various cake-box recipes.

'I mean, who can say no to free champers and cake, right?!' she'd said with a grin.

Kate and Ethel had both agreed that it was a great idea - but that had been when it had been a theory rather than a reality. But the incredible summer weather they were experiencing in Seabury brought a wave of new visitors to the town - and as most of them were staying with Veronica at The Pebble Street Hotel, they invariably ended up at The Sardine for a much needed second breakfast - and tended to come back for lunch as well.

Kate had now lost count of the number of times she'd been asked if they did evening meals at The Sardine, and she was starting to seriously consider it as an option.

'One new idea at a time!' was Ethel's wise warning the day before, when she'd floated the idea past her.

Kate couldn't blame her. Ethel's workload had just skyrocketed due to the cake-box plan - and she was in full-flow, perfecting the samples for the party on Saturday night.

Sarah, who'd proven herself to be the perfect right-hand-man for Ethel on the baking front, had begged for the previous day off. She'd been invited to go shopping with her friends over in Plymouth, followed by what sounded like a very giggly, girly sleepover. Of course, Kate had agreed immediately. Trixie was still out of action, so Kate had covered the café herself, leaving Ethel free to obsess about tweaking cake recipes.

'Usual, Lionel?' said Kate as he strode into the café with a beaming smile.

'Yes please! No Sarah again - is she well?'

'She's due in any moment!' said Kate, firing up the Italian Stallion for what already felt like the thousandth time that morning. 'She had a well-earned day off to hang out with her friends yesterday, and she'll be in to help Ethel with more party preparations this afternoon, while I man the fort here.'

'Jolly good!' said Lionel. 'I've grown quite fond of

that little firecracker already. Shame her father's such a... well, you know.'

Kate bit down on an uncomfortable smile. 'I hate to say it, but I don't think he's quite as bad as he seemed at first.'

'How so?' demanded Lionel. 'Charlie told me about your accident. Surely you haven't forgiven him for hurting our boy?' he said, laying his hand on Stanley's head - because, of course, he was already under the table. Stanley knew that if Lionel was here, that meant toast-treats at any moment.

'Well, I'm afraid I was mistaken there,' said Kate, now feeling decidedly awkward. 'It wasn't him driving. Apparently, it was his rather unsavoury ex-wife.'

'Oh. Well! That's quite a turn up for the books.'

Kate nodded, piling Lionel's toast onto a plate and bringing it over to his table.

'Thank you,' he said with a grateful nod. 'Well, I do have to say that I'm relieved in a way - it felt pretty uncomfortable having someone that inconsiderate living with us here in Seabury.'

Kate nodded again. She knew what he meant. Her own feelings about Mike Pendle were now so muddled, she didn't know what to think. On one hand, he'd been so concerned to hear that Stanley had been hurt that he'd called the vet himself to check up on him and then anonymously covered the bill. But, on the other hand, he'd complained to the council about The Sardine and had her outdoor tables removed. Add to that the fact that he'd generally been a bit of a... well, a bit of a Grumpy Badger about Sarah... she really didn't know what to think anymore.

The picture Sarah had painted was of a kind and considerate father who she'd actively wanted to live with after the divorce. A little strict and blinkered when it came to the possibilities for her future perhaps, but certainly a parent who doted on his daughter.

'Earth to Kate?' laughed Lionel.

'Sorry Lionel!'

'Where were you, anywhere nice?'

Kate smiled. 'Just trying to work out our Mr Pendle, if I'm honest. He's still a bit of an enigma!'

'Ah, the joys of new blood in a town as small as ours, eh?' chuckled Lionel, taking a sip of his coffee. 'Nothing like a new character to study.'

Kate nodded, wondering if she should tell him about the fact that Mike had paid Stanley's vet bill, but promptly decided against it. Something told her that he hadn't done it for praise and might not like that particular bit of information bandied around.

'So, have you asked him to the party?' said Lionel. 'Charlie and I can't wait!'

Kate's mouth dropped open. 'You know, I haven't,' she said, suddenly feeling bad. It wasn't that she'd actively decided against it, she just hadn't even considered it in the first place. 'How awful of me! I'll make sure I send an invitation back with Sarah this evening.'

'Good girl,' he said approvingly. 'You know, your

dad really would be proud of the woman you've become.'

Kate smiled at him. 'That means a lot. Though I somehow doubt he'd have approved quite so much if he'd seen me screaming at the poor guy after Stanley got hurt, and then calling him a grumpy badger last time I saw him!'

Lionel chuckled. 'Oh I don't know, even your gentle old dad could be quite peppery when roused.'

Kate laughed, nodding. She loved the fact that she lived in a town where every single local helped her to keep the memory of her wonderful dad alive. When he'd died, so many people had asked her if she was going to move away from Seabury "for a fresh start" and "to escape the memories" - but being here, where her history was known and cherished by so many people, was one of the biggest comforts of her life.

'So,' said Kate, plopping down into one of the empty chairs for a brief moment's respite, 'while she's not here, any gossip on the Ethel and Charlie front?'

'Only that I don't think I've seen Charlie smile so much in his entire life,' said Lionel, feeding Stanley a toast crust, which disappeared in record speed.

'But what's been said?' prodded Kate, excitedly. 'All I know is that he brought her the most beautiful bunch of flowers, Ethel went all mushy because he knew what her favourites were, they shared a pot of tea while Ethel had a break and that was that!'

Lionel shrugged. 'Yes, but it meant far more than that, I think. Ethel asked Charlie to the party.'

'Because I told her to!'

'Yes, but Charlie saw it as a sign - a good sign.'

'Well, I really hope he makes the next move, otherwise they're doomed to remain friends forever!' said Kate, shaking her hair back and heaving herself to her feet again.

'Would that be so bad?' asked Lionel.

'Not bad - but when they both love each other...'

'You think Ethel returns his feelings then?' asked Lionel, his eyes shining.

'Actually, yes - I do.'

'Then, my girl, we shall watch with interest, won't we?!'

'What'll we watch with interest?' demanded Sarah, bouncing into the café and promptly dropping to her knees to give Stanley his customary cuddle which he returned with interest. 'Morning gang!'

'Ah, there's our girl,' smiled Lionel. 'Just in time to make me coffee number two. I've got a painting to finish off today, so I need my go-go juice!'

'Coming right up,' said Sarah, hauling herself to her feet and heading to wash her hands. 'Anyway - what are we watching with interest?' she said again, going to the fridge for the milk and pouring it into a frother jug.

'Oh... erm...' hedged Lionel.

'Just which cake combinations will prove to be the favourites at the party!' invented Kate quickly.

'My money's on the rhubarb streusel cupcakes!' said Sarah. 'They're still my faves.'

The landline started to ring, making Kate jump. The thing virtually never rang, and the sound sent a nervous thrill through her for some reason.

'Sarah, mind doing a quick tour around the yard to check everyone's okay once you've done that?' she asked, reaching for the receiver.

Sarah gave her the thumbs up, delivered Lionel's fresh coffee, then headed straight outside.

'Well, that's good news - in a way,' said Kate, replacing the receiver just as Sarah strode back into the café with three new orders to work through.

'What's happened?' she asked.

'Trixie'll be ready to pick up on Friday.'

'How's that "in a way" - surely that's brilliant news?'

'Well yeah - but typical because we've got the party the day after, so I'll have nowhere to park her!'

'Just bung her on the pavement outside until we're done!' shrugged Sarah.

Kate huffed. 'Not with-' she stopped abruptly, looking awkward. 'Not with the *council* looking to find fault,' she amended quickly. She'd been about to bad-mouth Mike, and she'd sworn not to do that in front of her.

'Okay,' said Sarah, 'so park her in one of the spots in

front of dad's place. They're public spaces, and she should be safe there - you've got a chain for her and that weird lock thing for the trailer, haven't you?'

Kate nodded. She hadn't even thought about one of the public parking spots. They were free... but it really was *super* cheeky to park right outside her new rival, wasn't it?!

'Wouldn't your dad mind?' she said.

Sarah shrugged. 'He's not even open yet. It won't be for long - and not like it's on his launch day or anything!'

'Sarah makes good points,' put in Lionel. 'I think you're worrying too much!'

Kate shrugged. 'Great. Well, that's sorted then!'

'Right ladies, I'm off. Give my best to Ethel when she comes in, tell her not to overdo it before the party! She's got to be fresh and all bright-eyed and bushy-tailed for her date with Charlie.'

Kate nodded. 'I'll give her your love - but there's no way I'm saying the rest of it - I value my life too highly!'

Lionel saluted, gave Stanley a last pat and they waved him off.

'Is Ethel okay?' asked Sarah.

Kate nodded. 'She's fine - may be getting a *little* bit stressed. She missed your help yesterday, I think.'

'God, I'm really sorry,' said Sarah looking anxious.

'No, I didn't mean it like that! You deserved a day off after everything you've been doing! What I meant was - I think you two make an excellent team. But I do think we need to consider another member of staff, don't you?'

Sarah cocked her head thoughtfully and then nodded. 'Yep. I mean Ethel's amazing, but she's only meant to be doing your cakes and just occasionally helping out, isn't she? And she's been pretty much full-time since I started.'

Kate nodded. Sarah was right. Ethel was so feisty and quick to offer her help, it was too easy to forget that she was in her seventies. She'd taken on a lot to help her out - especially since the accident - but Kate didn't want to take advantage of her.

'Let's get this party over and done with and then I'll start looking for someone else. I got way too lucky with you, you know - you breezed in and spoilt us!'

Sarah blushed and kicked the heel of her converse against the floor. 'Thanks, Kate.'

Kate gave her a friendly nudge with her elbow.

'One thing,' said Sarah, 'when you do get someone new - make sure they're into baking too.'

Kate raised her eyebrows. 'Really? Surely that's your thing... and I'd never replace Ethel's cakes...'

'Yeah - but if you want the cake boxes to take off, it just makes sense to bring in someone who's at least got a passion for that side of things. I mean, even if you decide against carrying on with the cake subscriptions at some point - a baker's never going to go to waste here, are they? Plus - it's an added bonus for me if there's someone else's brain to pick!' she laughed.

'Okay, you've got it!' said Kate. 'So, how was your sleepover?'

'Epic!' grinned Sarah. 'It was like being a little kid again. We got pizzas and pick'n'mix and did face masks and watched cartoons!'

'You're not a normal teenager, are you? You're an alien!'

Sarah giggled. 'The only gross bit was when Tina's mum came home. We were all hanging out in the living room, and she didn't realise, and her and her boyfriend came in glued to each other's faces like limpets!'

Kate snorted. 'Did they see you?'

'Only when Tina started making puking sounds. I think they'd have ended up naked before they realised there were six teenagers in the room otherwise. Then they disappeared upstairs. One guess where they were going!' she paused for a moment and sighed. 'Tina hates it. This guy just drops in like once a week and then disappears, and then turns up again when he wants another shag. She thinks he's using her mum because she's a bit... you know... vulnerable. Because Tina's dad left.'

'That sounds horrible!' said Kate.

Sarah shrugged. 'Total slimeball. Made me feel really lucky that dad's pretty cool. He'd never do something like that.'

'Ooh - well reminded!' said Kate. 'Sorry to change the subject, but before I forget, would you mind if I invite your dad to the party?'

Sarah smiled at her. 'No. Course not. Actually, I bet he'll be chuffed. Ever since he found out I work here, he won't shut up about you.'

Kate's smile froze on her face. 'What do you mean?' she asked, trying to keep her tone light.

'Oh, you know - tons and tons of questions! Don't worry - I never tell him anything.'

'Right,' muttered Kate as Sarah rushed off to serve a couple of women who'd just come in.

She couldn't believe it. He'd been so worried about the possibility of Sarah discussing New York Froth with her - now here *he* was, questioning Sarah about The Sardine! So much for grumpy badger - hypocritical badger might be closer to the mark. And now she'd told Sarah about inviting him to the party, there was no way she could do a U-turn.

Balls. Bloody Mike Pendle had struck again.

CHAPTER 15

'Paula - you're early!' said Kate, rushing over to give her friend a hug then realising that she was still carrying a pile of Tupperware. 'Two secs,' she laughed, heading into the yard and handing the boxes over to Sarah.

She couldn't believe how fast the weekend had arrived, but now that the party was almost here, Kate was a mixture of anxiety and excitement. She quickly handed over the last batch of cakes to Sarah, who was busy setting up the stands and setting out the goodies - one variety per table - along with voting slips so that everyone could leave comments and vote on their favourites.

'Right - come here,' she said, turning back to Paula and pulling her into a massive hug. As she stepped back, Kate subtly looked her friend up and down. She was pretty sure she'd lost weight, but at least she looked alert and a lot healthier than she had a couple of weeks ago. 'You're looking gorgeous!' she said.

'Thanks, Kate,' said Paula, giving her a soft smile. 'So - who're you expecting this evening? Blimey, it looks like you've invited half the town if those piles of cakes are anything to go by.'

'Half the town?' laughed Kate, 'I think I invited pretty much the *whole* town, to be honest!'

'Of course you did,' chuckled Paula. 'That's so like you!'

Kate shrugged. 'Well - I think everyone from the allotments is coming, all the Chilly Dippers of course, Veronica, Lionel, some of the town councillors-'

'Good move,' said Paula, pinching one of Sarah's now-famous apple macarons off the top of the nearest pyramid and taking a bite. 'Oh my sainted aunts - that's *heavenly!*'

'Sarah's a genius!' said Kate with a shrug.

'Really good call on inviting the council though - shows no hard feelings on the whole table licence thing.'

'Yeah, well,' said Kate frowning, 'I should have made sure I'd covered my backside, shouldn't I? I've invited Mike Pendle too,' she added in a low voice so that Sarah didn't hear her.

'You have?' said Paula. 'That's very forgiving of you!'

'Have to admit I regretted it pretty much straight away.'

'Well - he's part of the town now. You may as well try and get on, right?'

Kate nodded. 'That's basically what Lionel said too.'

'Well - he's pretty wise,' she grinned.

'Yeah, but Sarah said he's been asking loads of questions about The Sardine!' muttered Kate.

'But you've got nothing to hide.'

Kate stared at her friend for a second then laughed. 'Trust you to give me a new perspective so easily. You're right! Thanks.'

'You're welcome! Hey, Kate... do you reckon we could go for a walk, just us two - and Stanley, of course - and maybe have a bit of a picnic? Soon?'

Kate frowned at her friend, a spike of concern going through her again. It wasn't that she didn't want to spend more time with her friend - of *course* she did. But the way she'd just asked felt so... formal.

Paula laughed. 'Don't look at me like that! You've just been mega-busy recently, and the selfish being that I am - I'd really like some "Kate-time"' she grinned.

'You know, I'd really love that,' said Kate, nodding. 'You're right, we've barely had a chance to chat, have we? Time just seems to disappear, doesn't it?'

Paula nodded, and Kate could swear that a tiny flash of sadness crossed her friend's face before being quickly replaced by another smile.

'Now - what can I do to help,' asked Paula.

'Just chill?' said Kate, knowing full-well this wouldn't cut it.

'Kate Hardy - give me a job to do this instant!'

'Okay, okay!' laughed Kate, holding up her hands in surrender. 'Well, if you wouldn't mind - could you pop into the kitchen and check if Ethel needs a hand with anything, while I help Sarah finish off out here? I need to get the champagne glasses lined up and ready to roll!'

'You've got it!' said Paula, giving her a quick kiss on the cheek before heading towards The Sardine to check on Ethel.

Kate knew that the older woman would have everything perfectly under control - as usual - but she might welcome an extra pair of hands, nonetheless.

She made her way over to Sarah, who shot her a quick grin before looking back down at the paper napkin she was folding. She'd finished setting out the cakes, and the gorgeous stands with their mountains of sweet treats looked really rather special. Kate couldn't wait to see what everyone's favourites were.

'Paula loved your apple macarons!' she said, settling in to help Sarah.

'Yay!'

'Where's Stanley?' Kate asked, glancing around. Sarah had been left to keep an eye on him as Kate had been rushing back and forth between the kitchen and the yard for the past hour or so, ferrying boxes and tables, chairs and cake stands, and bottle after bottle of champagne.

Sarah pointed to the corner, and Kate looked over

and spotted a pair of furry hind legs sticking out from behind one of the trestle tables.

'He had a good snuffle around, checked for any crumbs we'd missed, and now he's having a pre-party nap,' laughed Sarah.

'Gathering his strength - he'll be petted to within an inch of his life later,' laughed Kate, 'but on the plus side, we won't have many cake crumbs to clear up afterwards! Oh crikey, I hadn't thought - will your dad be okay with Stanley being here?'

'I guess he'll just have to keep his distance,' said Sarah.

'It's such a shame,' said Kate quietly.

'Yeah,' said Sarah, grabbing another napkin and folding it carefully. 'See, his dad - my grandad - really wasn't a nice guy. Used to own this Alsatian when dad was a kid, and it sounds like he was absolutely vile to it. Made it really aggressive. Then if dad was ever naughty, he'd basically use the dog to punish him.'

Kate froze, a look of horror on her face. 'You're joking?' she said.

Sarah shrugged. 'He didn't make it actually attack him, I don't think,' said Sarah, 'but he'd send dad to his room and then basically set the dog at the open door to stand guard. If dad got too close, it would snarl and snap - bare its teeth - that sort of thing.'

'No wonder he reacted badly when he first saw Stanley.'

Sarah shrugged again. 'It's not so bad if he gets

some warning. Like, he knows Stanley might be around tonight, so he'll be expecting it and will have the chance to prepare.'

'But he *is* definitely coming?' said Kate.

Sarah nodded. 'I think he's looking forward to it. Hopefully, he might have stopped muttering about Trixie by then,' she laughed.

'Ah. So - the parking spot didn't go down too well then?' said Kate, pulling a face.

'Not so much - as we expected. Nothing he can do about it though, is there?!' said Sarah.

'I'll be sure to tell him I won't make a habit of it once he's open,' laughed Kate.

'I wouldn't worry - he'll be on his best behaviour tonight. He's probably pretty nervous.'

'Nervous?' laughed Kate. 'Your dad?'

'You know, I still think you might have the wrong impression about him,' said Sarah quietly.

Kate wasn't sure what to say. She really didn't want to upset Sarah.

'Well, it'll be nice to have him here,' she said, hoping it was a gentle full-stop on the conversation for now. Because, really, Kate no longer knew what to think about Mike Pendle, and every time he was mentioned a strange little fluttering sensation hit her in the chest. She had no idea if it was caused by a bit of left-over anger towards him or... perhaps something a bit more troubling!

Half of her was still livid with him for being an

interfering, council-dobbing know-it-all, and the other half now really felt for the scared little boy Sarah had just told her about. And - even though the maths didn't add up - the third half of her admired his generosity and his love for his daughter. Mike Pendle was a conundrum.

~

'Thank you all so much for coming!' said Kate, addressing the crowd filling their little yard. She usually hated any kind of public speaking, but this was different. Yes, there were so many people crammed in here that they spilled out onto the pavement - but every single person here was familiar to her. This was her family - her beloved Seabury - who'd come out en masse to support her.

'I'm not going to keep you. Go forth and drink all the bubbly, try all the cakes, and don't forget to leave us your comments and vote for your favourites. You'll be able to sign up for one of our weekly cake subscription boxes or treat yourself to a cream-tea pack - from Monday!'

A massive cheer went up, complete with loud pops as Charlie and Ethel sent the corks flying on a couple of fresh bottles of bubbly. Kate was about to go over and give them a hand to pass out the glasses when she felt a hand on her arm. She turned to find a short, rather dumpy woman with a shock of white-blond hair and bright fuchsia lipstick smiling at her.

'Councillor Jones!' said Kate in surprise. 'So glad you could make it.' She'd invited all of the town councillors, but she'd hardly expected any of them to turn up.

'Well, thank you for inviting me!' said the councillor, bending over to ruffle Stanley's ears. 'Hello boy!' she crooned. 'I heard about your accident. He's all better I hope?' she asked, straightening back up.

'Yes - he's fine now, thank goodness.'

'Good. So - congratulations on your wonderful new ideas,' she said. 'I've already tested the macarons, the mini-fudge-flapjacks and, of course, I'm no stranger to Ethel's scones!' she laughed. 'You can count on me as one of your first customers.'

Kate smiled warmly at her. 'Thank you so much. I really appreciate your support.'

'Not at all - I love my cake,' she laughed. 'And it will be a real boon for the town too. Now then, have you thought about building your social media presence?' she demanded.

Kate shook her head, feeling slightly bewildered. 'Not really. All my customers are locals, other than the random visitors who stumble in, of course!'

'Well - you should. It would be great for The Sardine and could bring more visitors to the town too, make it a bit of a destination... think about it!'

Kate nodded. The idea made her shudder slightly,

but maybe there *wouldn't* be any harm in sharing a few photographs of her favourite place in the entire world - and mix in a bit of cakey-goodness while she was at it!

'Okay - I'll have a chat with the others and see what they think.'

'Wonderful. Oh, and Kate,' said the councillor, now eyeing a mountain of gooey chocolate brownies on a nearby table, 'the licence for your outdoor seating is in the post. Should be with you on Monday.'

Kate beamed at her. She might not be *quite* so desperate for it now that she had the yard set up, but it would be good to have that spot back too. Her two little tables under the awning had been there ever since she'd first opened the café. Now that Trixie was back in action as well, it really felt like everything was falling into place again.

'Thank you,' she said warmly.

'Congratulations again,' smiled the councillor. 'The Sardine is a real asset to Seabury, as are you.'

Kate watched her move away towards the brownies, then bent down to give Stanley a hug.

'Hear that, boy?' she whispered, burying her face in his soft fur for a moment. 'We're an asset.'

'Don't get used to it. They're a fickle bunch.'

The voice from above made Kate's jaw clench in spite of her happy mood. She stood back up and plastered a fake smile on her face.

'Veronica,' she said. 'Thanks for coming.'

Veronica simply sniffed.

'Do help yourself to a glass of bubbly,' said Kate.

'I don't drink that cheap supermarket stuff,' she huffed.

'Oh,' said Kate, and watched as Stanley disappeared off through the crowd again, making his way determinedly towards Ethel and Charlie who were busy chatting in the corner with eyes for no one but each other. She forced her attention back to Veronica. 'Well, this stuff's from that vineyard over near Little Bamton, but if you don't like it, I'm sure Sarah can help you to some elderflower bubbly instead.'

'I'll wait until I get home, thanks. I just wanted to let you know that I think your idea is ridiculous. All style, no substance,' she said, pointing at one of the cardboard cake boxes that Kate had had printed up with The Sardine's logo. Each one had six little inner compartments, all ready for the individual cakes to sit in.

'I'm sorry you feel that way,' said Kate, fighting not to roll her eyes. She loved her new cake boxes, and she was buggered if she was going to let this miserable old trout spoil such a happy evening.

'Smells of desperation, Kate, to be honest. Though I *do* understand where you're coming from. I'd be worried too if I were you. I guarantee the minute New York Froth opens up, you'll be out of business.'

'Well, *do* be sure to support Mike when he opens, won't you? Life's about supporting each other, after all,' she said with a syrupy smile. Kate couldn't actually remember the last time Veronica had spent a single penny at The Sardine, and she'd be more than happy if she never appeared in the café ever again. 'Enjoy your evening' she added smoothly.

Veronica, however, didn't seem to want to take the hint to clear off. Instead, she grabbed at one of the nearest lemon-drizzle cupcakes - complete with exquisite icing piped on by Ethel (watched closely by Sarah) - and shoved half of it in her mouth, chewing noisily.

'You'll never make this stick,' she said, swallowing, then pursing her mouth into a little cat's bum. 'Too expensive. Too *look at me.*' She paused, took another bite then shook her head. 'Honestly, you don't have a clue what you're doing here do you? Thank heavens I told the council you didn't have a permit for those tables outside - you could have got into some real trouble there.'

'I'm sorry - *what*?!' spluttered Kate.

'Those blasted tables you had outside, cluttering the pavement. Honestly! Much safer without them. Though,' she said, licking the remaining icing from her fingers while Kate winced at the sight, '*why* Mike suggested you use this yard instead is anyone's guess. Not the sharpest knife in the drawer, that one! Seems his ex-wife was the brains in that outfit!'

With her piece said, Veronica wandered off at last. Kate balled her hands into fists as she watched Veronica load cake after cake into a serviette then place them into her capacious handbag. Kate would bet pretty much anything that they'd be served up at The Pebble Street Hotel the next day.

Right now though, Kate didn't really care. Her whole world felt like it had just shifted on its axis. *Veronica* had set the council on her? *Mike* had been the one to come up with the idea of using the yard? What was this world coming to?

She looked around her, desperate for someone to talk to - someone who'd help her make sense of these strange things - and came face to face with Mike.

CHAPTER 16

'Congratulations. This place looks amazing,' he said with a smile.

Kate opened her mouth to thank him but paused.

'Kate? Are you okay?'

'This was your idea?' she said, sounding like she was surfacing from deep water.

'Huh?'

'Using the yard as extra seating for The Sardine was your idea?' she said in a low voice.

Mike shrugged. 'Well, yeah, I might have mentioned in passing that it seemed like a good idea.'

'But you didn't even know Sarah was working for me when she surprised me with the idea!'

'No, I know. But I said something about it to her when we went for a stroll together around the town one evening,' he laughed. 'I'd noticed that you hadn't put the tables outside that day, Sarah muttered something about the council stopping you, and I said I was surprised you didn't make better use of Trixie's yard. That's all there was to it'

'Oh...' Kate shook her head, looking like she was trying to clear water from her ears as she struggled to get her head around this.

'I promise, it wasn't anything weirder than that. It was Sarah who ran with the idea. And it's worked out brilliantly by the looks of it - though I *would* be happier if you'd chosen literally *anywhere* else to dump Trixie.'

Kate let out a snort of laughter. 'Don't worry - I promise that's a one-off unless I really need to torture you for something!'

'Much obliged!' said Mike with a little nod.

'Tell me, though,' said Kate, 'how *exactly* did Veronica know it was your idea to use the yard?'

Mike's face fell. 'Well, I picked her brain a bit when I first arrived.'

'Yes, I know. She told me you'd taken her to lunch.'

'The one and only time I'll ever fall into that trap,' he muttered. 'Anyway, I was trying to find out more about you after I'd blocked your yard that first morning - so I asked her about you. I think I might have asked her about the yard too.'

'So, you were trying to get the inside scoop on the enemy, hey?' said Kate, her voice coming out a bit harsher than she'd intended.

Mike raised his eyebrows and shook his head. 'No. Just trying to find out more about the beautiful woman who was single-handedly running a thriving business in such a small town - the one who was more than a little bit fiery.'

Kate's mouth dropped open and she watched as Mike flushed. It *was* quite packed in here - but she was pretty sure that was a blush rather than him being too hot. *What* was going on here this evening?!

'Erm - is Stanley around?' he asked, clearing his throat and awkwardly changing the subject.

'Yes - but it's okay - he headed over to Ethel and... oh, goodness!' she said with a gasp. Her eyes had sought Ethel in the crowd only to find her standing with Charlie's arm around her shoulders.

'Well, looks like those two are getting on!' said Mike with a gentle smile.

'It does, doesn't it!' said Kate. 'Anyway, you're still safe - Stanley's over with Sarah,' she added, giving Sarah a little wave and getting a thumbs-up in return. It looked like she'd clipped Stanley's lead on to keep him with her. Thoughtful girl.

'It's okay,' said Mike. 'I actually brought him something... I'd really like to... well, to get to know him a bit better. If that's okay, of course?'

Kate watched as Mike reached inside his posh suit jacket and drew out a brown paper bag. He handed it over to her. Inside it was a large, knotted hide-bone.

'Mike!' she said in surprise, 'this is so kind of you!'

'Well,' he said, looking a bit embarrassed, 'I thought he might like it to wash down all the cake.'

'He'll love it. Do you want to give it to him yourself?'

Mike shook his head. 'Nah, I'll leave it for you. But I meant what I said, I really *would* like to get to meet him properly - but maybe when things are a bit quieter?'

'Come here!' said Kate, and without thinking about it too hard, she reached forward and drew a very surprised Mike Pendle into a warm hug.

After a second, Kate felt him relax against her. Mike's arms softened around her, drawing her closer. Kate felt something deep inside her chest shift. She didn't want this hug to end - she didn't want to draw away from him.

'You know,' said Mike quietly in her ear, 'I'd really like to get to know you better too... maybe I could take you up on that offer of finding out how things *really* work here in Seabury?'

Kate pulled back and his eyes locked onto hers. There seemed to be something warm and hopeful in his face, and for just a second, it was like someone had hit the mute button on the sounds of the party going on around them. For just a second, she wondered if he was going to kiss her... or maybe... if she was going to kiss him...

'Kate?'

The low, accented male voice made her jump away from Mike as if she'd received an electric shock.

'Pierre?' she squeaked, trying to smooth her hair back away from her face, then realising she was waving the paper bag with Stanley's bone around wildly in the process. She shoved it into her pocket. 'Erm, hi! This is a... surprise!'

'So I see,' he said, raising his eyebrows and shooting a look from her to Mike.

'No - oh, noooo!' she laughed, the giggle sounding a little manic. 'This is Mike. He's opening a café over on North Beach. He was just giving me the bone... I mean, *a* bone - for Stanley.'

Kate was gabbling and she knew it. She shot a quick look at Mike, who appeared to be struggling to swallow a giggle. She looked around her for help, only to find Sarah staring at her across the yard, a horrified look on her face.

Ah shit - had Sarah just spotted what happened with her dad? Or what *almost* happened...

'Good to meet you,' said Mike, holding out his hand to shake Pierre's. 'You are?'

'Kate's boyfriend,' replied Pierre, not taking Mike's hand but instead winding his arm protectively around Kate's shoulders and kissing the top of her head.

'Oh. Right,' said Mike, the smile dropping from his face. 'Erm, I should... erm... cake,' he pointed over towards Sarah and moved away through the crowd as fast as he could.

Kate stared after him in surprise. *What exactly* was happening here? She craned her neck to look over at Sarah again. She needed to check that she was okay - but Pierre had her clamped to his side.

'You are not happy to see me?' he laughed, clearly not believing a word of it.

Kate looked back to him and gave him a little smile. 'Of course I am - just surprised! I didn't even know you were in the country!'

'I could not go too long without seeing you again,' he said, pulling her around and landing a huge kiss right on her lips.

Kate couldn't help it, she squirmed away from him slightly. She really wasn't particularly keen on canoodling in public - especially at what was essentially a work do.

'What? You go off me?' he said, with a fake pout.

'Course not,' said Kate in a low voice, shaking her head. 'But I have guests.'

'It is someone's birthday?'

'No - we're taste-testing cakes and launching a new bit of my business.'

'So, it's work,' he said with a nod.

Kate felt her shoulders relax a bit. He understood. Thank heavens for that.

'Yes, it's work,' she smiled.

'So - you can hand over to your staff and come away with me!' he said, getting a firmer grasp on her waist and pulling her so close to him it almost hurt.

'I can't!' she said, with a light laugh. Again, she struggled away from him. 'Sorry. We've been planning this for a while - it's too important!'

'So, you don't want to spend time with me?'

This was getting ridiculous. Kate struggled to reign in her growing impatience. This wasn't how it was meant to work between the two of them! She thought they had an understanding.

Of course, he *was* welcome - but welcome to eat cake, chat to her friends and *let her get on with her business!* He wasn't welcome to try guilt-tripping her out of her own party just because he'd decided to turn up out of the blue. But right now wasn't the moment to tackle that particular problem. Not in front of the whole of Seabury!

'Look,' she said, forcing a smile onto her face, 'let's just-'

'Ooh Kate!' said Paula, materialising at her side and eyeballing Pierre. 'Is this your mystery man? Are you going to introduce us?'

Perfect. Paula to the rescue!

'Pierre, this is my best friend Paula. Paula - Pierre.'

'Enchante!' said Pierre, grabbing Paula's hand and kissing the back of it.

'Oh my,' she giggled.

Kate rolled her eyes good-naturedly. Pierre *did* tend to have that effect. She remembered it well.

'Paula - can you help Pierre to some bubbly and your favourite cake?'

'But chérie-' Pierre began to argue.

'I'll be right back!' said Kate, struggling to stop an eye roll from slipping out. 'I just need to check in with Ethel and Sarah!'

Kate headed over towards where Ethel and Charlie were still standing in the corner. They didn't seem to have budged all evening, and Kate hated to break into their cosy little bubble, but she really did need to check Sarah was okay. She couldn't see her or Mike anywhere.

'Hello love!' said Ethel, her eyes sparkling.

'Hi you two!' she said. 'Having fun?'

'A lovely evening,' grinned Charlie. 'Thank you for all the cake.'

Kate smiled and watched as Charlie took hold of Ethel's hand. She wanted nothing more than to find out *exactly* how this miracle had come about, but first, she had to check that Sarah wasn't too freaked out by witnessing the almost-whatever-it-had-nearly-been between her and Mike. Before Pierre had interrupted.

'Good. Good. I'm glad,' she said distractedly. 'Have you seen Sarah?'

'Didn't she find you?' said Ethel.

Kate shook her head. 'No, why?'

'She's had to go. Wasn't feeling well. Mike took her home I think.'

'Oh *no!*' said Kate. This was not good.

'She had a sudden headache or something,' said Ethel. 'She *has* been working hard, and between you and me I think she might have got a bit overexcited by the whole thing. Looked very pale and couldn't hold back the tears when Mike came to the rescue.'

Kate pulled a face. Headache? Yeah right. Total

horror was more like it. 'Maybe I should go over, or call Mike, or-'

Charlie shook his head. 'She'll be okay, don't worry. She's with her dad. I'm sure he'll let you know if it's anything serious.'

'But-'

'Kate?'

Kate clenched her teeth. *God save her from clingy Frenchmen!*

'Pierre,' she said, turning to him.

'Are you ready to come away now?'

'No. I told you, I-'

'Pierre?' said Charlie, a massive grin spreading across his face. 'So you're Kate's chap?'

Pierre held out his hand and shook Charlie's.

'Pierre,' said Kate, feeling forced into it, 'this is Ethel who bakes all the cakes for The Sardine and works with me, and this is Charlie-'

'Ethel's chap!' said Charlie, pride beaming from his face.

Kate raised a delighted eyebrow at Ethel, who gave her a little shrug, unable to keep a huge smile from spreading across her own face.

'Delighted to meet you both,' said Pierre. 'I had hoped to... how do you say... whisk Kate away? But she will not be moved.'

'Well, no, I should think not,' said Ethel a tight little laugh. 'I'm not tidying this lot up on my own.'

'No fear of that, don't worry,' said Kate, rolling her

eyes at Ethel, who had to hide her expression behind her hand. 'Erm, have you guys seen Stanley? Last time I saw him Sarah had him on a lead to keep him away from Mike!'

'Well, you won't believe this, but Mike himself took the lead from Sarah and managed to hand him over to Doreen from the post office to look after. Last time I saw him they were sitting at that table over there with Councillor Jones,' said Ethel, pointing at the table closest to the gate.

Kate nodded. 'I'll be back in a bit,' she muttered, and feeling slightly guilty for dumping Pierre on Ethel and Charlie, scooted through the crowd to check on Stanley.

CHAPTER 17

Kate glanced down at her watch and sighed. It was only just gone nine in the evening, so why did she feel so exhausted?

'You look like I feel!' laughed Ethel, stacking the last few empty Tupperware boxes onto the trestle table. There had been very little cake left over by the end of the party, and she'd sent anything left home with the stragglers to enjoy tomorrow.

'Knackered?' laughed Kate.

Ethel nodded. 'But it was good, wasn't it?'

'Well, these certainly say so,' said Kate with a weary smile, wafting the huge stack of completed comment sheets at her. 'I'm looking forward to having a good look through them tomorrow. Thank you so much for helping tonight!' she added gratefully.

'I wouldn't have missed it for the world,' said Ethel

lightly. 'Hey, where's your man and Stanley? Didn't they fancy helping with the clear up?'

Kate shook her head as she tucked the forms carefully into a plastic folder, then glanced around at the yard. Not too bad. The rest of this could just wait until tomorrow.

'I sent them upstairs while you were saying your goodbyes to Charlie,' she said, watching Ethel as she squirmed slightly. 'Stanley - because I think one more cake crumb would have made him explode, and Pierre - because he was doing my head in!'

'Really?' said Ethel lightly. 'He seemed quite charming, in an... *insistent* sort of way.'

'That's one way of putting it!' sighed Kate. 'I don't know. Maybe it was just because I wasn't expecting him here tonight, or because he seemed to think I'd just drop everything because he'd turned up - but, well...' she stopped and made a frustrated gesture.

Ethel winked at her. 'Well, go easy on him. Or not. What did Sarah say to me the other day... oh yes - *you do you.*'

Kate snorted. 'We'll see. Anyway, I just needed a couple of moments to sort everything out down here and say goodbye to everyone properly, without tripping over him every time I turned around.'

Ethel nodded. 'Fair enough. Now then, is there anything else I can do?'

'Yes,' said Kate, stifling a yawn, 'you can take this,' she grabbed one of the last bottles of bubbly and handed it to her. 'Take it home, pop it in the fridge, and share it with your new man when you fancy it.'

'*New man*,' breathed Ethel, shaking her head. 'Who'd have thought?!'

Kate grinned at her. She seemed to be floating on cloud nine. 'Actually - I think the whole of Seabury's been waiting for it to happen.'

'Thanks Kate. We'll enjoy this - maybe with some strawberries up at the allotments' said Ethel, placing the bottle carefully into her bag and hoisting the whole thing onto her shoulder.

'Oh hush,' said Kate. 'You're making me jealous!'

'Hardly! You've got your very own international man of mystery waiting for you upstairs - and tomorrow's Sunday. Anything could happen!'

'Maybe,' said Kate. She didn't want to put a dampener on Ethel's mood by telling her that somehow, she didn't think Pierre was going to be around by tomorrow morning.

Waving her friend off, Kate summoned her last ounce of energy to haul the heavy gate to the yard closed. She would just shut the remainder of the party away for tonight and finish off the tidy up in the morning.

She clicked the padlock closed and then paused to stare out to sea for a moment, listening to the peaceful waves as they lapped at the golden sand of West Beach. If only she could take Stanley for a gentle wander along the shore to finish her evening off, rather than having to retreat to her flat and deal with the attentions of a weirdly clingy Pierre!

'Kate!'

The sharp call made her turn, only to find Mike striding towards her.

'Mike!' she said in surprise. 'Hi! Is Sarah okay? I wanted to check with you earlier, but-'

'She's in pieces!' he said, his face deadly serious and a frown firmly in place.

'Oh no! Is she really ill or...' she wasn't sure how to put this next bit, 'erm - did she spot us?'

'Us?' he said, confused.

'You know... whatever almost... nearly happened.'

'What, Kate? What nearly happened?'

He'd come to a halt so close to her that she could feel the heat radiating off him. He'd changed and was now wearing jeans and a soft, slouchy grey tee shirt. The sight was doing something very strange to her. She swallowed, doing her best to look him in the eye.

Did he *really* not know what she was talking about? Was it just her over-active imagination that had convinced her they would have kissed if Pierre hadn't turned up at exactly the wrong moment?

Or - *the right moment* - she quickly amended. Because she shouldn't be thinking about kissing Mike. He was her rival. Sarah's father. A grumpy badger.

No, she definitely shouldn't be thinking about kissing him, especially with him standing so close to her, waves of anger and worry rolling off him.

'Where's the arsehole, Kate?'

'Excuse me?' she said, taking a step back and crossing her arms protectively across her chest.

'The guy who turned up. Your lover!' he spat.

'Pierre?'

Mike nodded, and Kate watched in confusion as his anger suddenly and inexplicably seemed to drain from him again. 'Yeah, him,' he sighed.

'I don't get it. What's Pierre got to do with Sarah not feeling very well? Oh my... nothing *happened* did it? He didn't-?'

Mike quickly shook his head. 'Look, can we go up to your flat a minute?'

'No,' said Kate, 'Pierre's taken Stanley up for me. Just tell me what's going on, Mike!'

He sighed, running his hands through his hair. 'Okay, look. Sarah's met Pierre before.'

Kate shook her head, frowning, trying to make sense of this. 'Where?'

'At that sleepover she went to. Kate - he's the mum's *boyfriend*!'

Kate's mind started racing. The guy who'd been all over Sarah's friend's mum? 'He can't be, he lives in France,' she said.

'Well, apparently not. From what Sarah told me, he turns up every week or so - for a night or two.'

Kate swallowed, suddenly feeling sick.

And he turns up here about once or twice a month.

'Are you okay?' said Mike, reaching out a hand to

pat her on the arm, then thinking better of it and dropping it down next to his side again.

'EEEEW!' groaned Kate, giving a full-body shudder.

Mike's face went from anger to concern to slight amusement.

'And he's up in my flat!' she added, wringing her hands. 'Wait though - why did Sarah leave so suddenly?!'

'She couldn't tell you herself! She's terrified you'll hate her. I knew something was seriously wrong, but it took me ages to get the story out of her once we got home! I left her sobbing her heart out!'

'Why would I hate her?!' said Kate.

'Because she's worried she's just broken your heart!' said Mike. 'She said - if she hadn't been there and seen him-'

'Then I'd never have found out!' said Kate, giving another shudder of disgust. 'Tell her thank you. For saving me from - that! I'll tell her myself as soon as I get this... *situation*... under control.'

'So... you're okay?' asked Mike gently.

'I will be as soon as I get him out of my flat!' said Kate.

'Do you want me to stay? I can help,' said Mike, looking concerned.

'No,' said Kate. 'No - go back to Sarah.'

'You sure?' said Mike, uncertainty clouding his face. He was clearly torn between the desire to get back to make sure his daughter was okay and not wanting to leave Kate on her own to deal with Pierre.

Kate nodded. 'Seriously, go. Sarah's more important.'

'Okay - I will. Good luck!' he said, moving away from her as if to head back in the direction of North Beach. Then he paused and turned back to her. 'Look. Can you at least call me when you're done? I need to know he's gone and that you're okay. Come over afterwards if you want.'

Kate shook her head, knowing she wouldn't. 'I'll call you though,' she said.

'Here's my number,' said Mike, rummaging around in his pocket then handing her a decidedly crumpled business card.

'Okay,' she said, putting it in her pocket. 'And Mike - thank you!'

Mike shrugged, clearly still struggling with the idea of leaving her to deal with the mess alone.

'Seriously, go!' she laughed. 'I've got a letch to get out of my flat. Don't worry, Stanley will look after me.'

'Where's my dog?!' Kate demanded.

She'd shot straight up the stairs, wanting to get this scene over and done with before the pounding anger and disgust that was coursing through her system wore off and left her with the inevitable dollop of sadness that was bound to follow.

She'd just crashed into her little living room and stopped dead.

Pierre had lit every candle in the place, and the small room glowed with golden, flickering light. Pierre himself was stretched out on her squashy sofa, stark-bollock-naked.

Kate fought the urge to heave at the sight of him. He really *had* just turned up and expected sex, hadn't he? But then, why was she surprised? Clearly this was the way he operated. Right now, though - she had more important things to worry about. Stanley's bed was empty, and he was nowhere to be seen.

'Kate, chérie, come,' Pierre grinned, opening his arms.

Kate swallowed hard. 'Where. Is. My. Dog?!'

Pierre shrugged. 'I shut him in the Salle de Bain. Out of the way so we can-' he gestured at his lap.

'You did *what?!*' she said, desperately trying not to puke as she turned on her heel and headed back out into the hallway.

She could hear Stanley whining and scratching at the closed bathroom door on the next floor.

'It's okay, boy!' she called, running up the stairs. The sound of her voice was met with a loud thump. It sounded like Stanley had just thrown his whole weight at the door.

She flung it open, and Stanley flew out onto the

landing, burying his face in her front as she dropped to her knees and threw her arms around him.

'It's okay, boy,' she crooned into his fur. 'You're okay. I'm here.'

Stanley straightened up and started to lick her face, making Kate splutter.

'I'm okay, I'm okay, you idiot!' she laughed, trying to avoid being drowned by doggy kisses. 'Come on. Let's go and get rid of that bastard.'

She got to her feet headed back towards the stairs, flanked by Stanley. As she reached the top, Pierre appeared at the bottom, still without a stitch on.

'Kate, chérie - come!'

Kate pulled a face. 'You'd better cover *that* up,' she said in disgust, 'before I ask Stanley to remove it for you.'

Much to her amusement, Pierre took a step back, covering his privates with his hands.

'Get your shit together and get out,' said Kate, walking slowly down the stairs towards him.

Pierre backed away into the living room, not taking his eyes off of Stanley.

'Kate? I do not understand. I came to see you, so we could spend time together. I lit candles. I brought you presents...'

'How many others *are* there?' said Kate, tilting her head curiously as she followed him into the living room.

'Others?'

'Yes, *others* you little sh-!' Kate took a deep breath. 'I know there's at least one just along the coast who you visit a couple of times a week. Then there's me - a couple of times a month. That leaves *poor old Pierre* many lonely nights to fill, doesn't it?!'

She didn't expect an answer out of him, but it was quite satisfying to see a look of panic kindle in his eyes as he realised that he'd been busted.

'How... how did you-?'

'Oh, I have my spies,' snarled Kate.

Stanley took a couple of steps into the room, eyed his bed, and then ignoring it, continued to move towards Pierre.

'Get away from me!' said Pierre, taking another step backwards.

'*Wow!* said Kate, her mouth dropping open. 'Where'd your accent go?'

'Oh sod off!' he said, sounding about as English as it came. 'Like *you* didn't know. Deep down. It's all part of the mystique, innit?! All part of the *fantasy.*'

'Fantasy?' spluttered Kate.

'French fisherman? Bringing you sodding *fish?!* I mean, *Pierre?!*' he laughed. 'My name's Ian, you feckin' knob.'

Oh god oh god oh god!

She needed him out of here. She needed a shower. The longest, hottest shower in the entire world.

'Stanley?' said Kate, her voice shaking.

The big bear glanced up at her in concern, then

advanced on "Pierre" with the kind of low rumble Kate had never heard him make before.

Pierre took a terrified step backwards, his ankles caught on the base of the bookshelves and he let out a high-pitched squeal as his bare bum-cheeks got a bit too close to a candle for comfort.

'Get out get out get out GET OUT!' yelled Kate, grabbing his bundle of clothes off the floor and lobbing them at him.

Pierre caught them in a messy heap and finally took the hint. Clutching the bundle, he scrambled up and bounded over the sofa cushions to avoid having to get too close to Stanley, dropping one of his trainers in the process. He shot out of the room and down the stairs towards the front door, where he paused to yank his jeans on.

Kate grabbed the trainer and followed.

'GET OUT!' she yelled, lobbing the shoe at his head from the top of the stairs. Even in her rage, she couldn't help but be impressed with her aim.

That did it. "Pierre" fumbled with the door catch and promptly disappeared - half-dressed - out of her life.

CHAPTER 18

Kate stomped around the living room, snuffing out candles. She couldn't *believe* what had just happened! Another little shiver of disgust ran through her.

Ian? English Ian?!

What had he done - visited the fishmongers to buy something to bring her from his "boat" every time he came to see her?

Eeeeewwwww!

Kate threw open the sash window to let the soft salty evening air cleanse the room of *Ian* and the stink of candle smoke.

What else?

She looked around the room, searching for any remaining traces of his visit. Her eyes rested on the sofa cushions. Yuck. There was no way she was sitting on *them* until all vestiges of his bare, cheating buttcheeks had been washed off. She quickly stripped off the covers then took them straight through to the kitchen and bundled them into the washing machine.

Heading back into the living room, she knelt down next to Stanley, who'd been watching her with interest from his bed.

'You were *brilliant!*' she said, stroking his head. 'Oh - I nearly forgot...' she reached into her pocket and pulled out the paper bag Mike had given her earlier. 'This is from Mike. I think we like him, okay? What do you think?' she said, offering him the end of the bone.

Stanley sniffed it then took it gently from her.

'Thought so!' she laughed, as he settled down to give it a good chew. 'Actually, I'd better give him a call, hadn't I? Tell him you got rid of *Pierre,*' she sighed.

Kate struggled back to her feet and was about to plonk down onto the stripped sofa when she changed her mind and perched on the wooden bentwood chair by the open window instead.

Drawing out the card Mike had given her earlier, she flipped open her mobile.

'Uh oh,' she sighed. There were twelve missed calls and four new voicemails - all from the same number. A number she knew way too well. What did that plonker want from her now? Whatever it was, he could wait until she was in the mood to talk to him. Right now, she needed to call Mike.

But it was too late. Her phone lit up with a silent, incoming call. It was his number - again. Well - it wasn't like he could make her mood much worse than it already was!

'What?' she spat, answering the call.

'That's no way to speak to your husband!' slurred Tom's voice at the other end of the line.

Why oh why was she so bad at picking men?

'You're not my husband. At least, not for much longer,' she sighed.

'Kate. If you want this divorce to actually go through, you should start responding to my solicitor.'

Kate frowned. Tom sounded drunk. Very drunk. She really wasn't in the mood for this.

'Whatever. I sent the papers back.'

'You didn't respond to my solicitor,' he slurred again. 'You didn't answer the letter, Kate. And now it's going to be mine.'

He was starting to sound like a pantomime villain, he was that plastered. So why did something in what he just said send a tremor of fear through her? A letter? Shit. The letter!

The vague memory of an envelope being whipped out of her hand, folded and slipped into Ethel's apron pocket came back to her.

Shit, shit, shit! It was time to bluff.

'I've not received any letters,' she said.

'Well, that's your tough luck, isn't it?' he said. 'You had a week to respond.'

'To what?' she demanded.

'The Sardine!' he said.

Then there was a crash on the other end. It sounded like he'd just walked into something. Kate didn't particularly care. She was desperately trying to piece together whatever the hell he was trying to say.

'What are you on about?' she said.

'You need to sell The Sardine so that you can split it in the divorce. Or just give it to me.'

'Bullshit,' she said firmly, though she could now feel her hand trembling around her phone. 'This place is mine. I bought it with money from my dad's house. I owned it before we met.'

'And now you have to support me because we're getting divorced, and you've left me with nothing. Oops!'

There was another crash and a bit of swearing before he focused on her again.

'You deserted me, Kate. You owe me.'

'No - this has already been decided. The Sardine has nothing to do with the divorce.'

'Well, my solicitor says it does.'

'No!' she said again, feeling tears prick her eyes.

'Keep saying it,' he laughed. 'Won't make it come true. See you in court - *wifey*!'

The line went dead. Kate flung her phone away from her as she felt a weight land in her lap. Stanley had plonked himself down at her feet and rested his large head on her knees. She looked down at him, took a huge, shuddering breath... and then the dam broke.

Kate flopped forward and soaked her big bear's silky head with her tears.

The sound of hammering at the front door made Stanley bark and struggle away from Kate's tight cuddle. She'd lost track of how long the pair of them had been curled up together on the stripped sofa - her crying what felt like a never-ending river of tears into Stanley's coat. She wriggled into a more upright position as he jumped down and tilted his head, booming out another bark as another round of hammering started.

Kate roughly scrubbed at her sore, swollen eyes with her sleeve and peered down at her watch. Shit, it was really late. Who on earth was hammering at her door at this time of night?!

She got to her feet, wrapped her cardigan around her more snugly and headed down towards the door.

'Kate? Kate!' came a muffled call, followed by more hammering.

It was Mike. Crikey, he'd wake up the entire town if he carried on like that! She quickly opened the door.

'Mike... what...?'

'Oh, thank goodness! You didn't *bloody* call me - I had to check you were okay.'

'It's nearly midnight!' said Kate, rubbing her face again.

'I know it's nearly bloody midnight - I-' he paused. 'Oh shit, Kate. Did he hurt you?' he demanded, now staring at her swollen, tear-stained face. 'I *knew* I should have stayed. I'll get that little-'

'It's fine,' said Kate in a flat voice. 'He's long gone. Won't be back in a hurry either!'

'So - what's... I mean... you've been crying?' he said, his face creased with worry.

The words were like a switch. Kate's chin instantly started to quiver, and the tears started to fall again.

'Hey, hey - it's okay!' said Mike. He reached out and gently laid a hand on her shoulder. 'Do you want me to come up for a minute?' he asked, looking bewildered.

Kate nodded, then shook her head. 'Stanley!' she sobbed.

'What's happened to Stanley!' demanded Mike.

'No... Stanley's up... up there,' she sobbed.

'Oh. Well. That's okay. We had a chat earlier. We're cool!' said Mike, a determined set to his chin.

Kate couldn't do anything other than nod and turn to head back up the stairs. Mike followed her inside, closed the door behind him quietly and then trailed up the stairs behind her.

Stanley was standing at the living room door on lookout duty.

'It's okay boy,' said Kate, patting him on the head. 'Come on!'

Stanley eyed Mike, who'd paused at the top of the stairs.

'Hey, Stanley,' he said, holding out his hand.

Stanley stepped forward, sniffed Mike's hand, gave a soft wag of his tail then turned and retreated onto his bed.

Mike followed him into the living room, taking his time to look around the cosy space and admire Lionel's paintings. Kate watched him, trying to get a hold of herself and stop her tears from flowing. She had a sneaking suspicion he was trying to give her a moment to pull herself together.

'Gorgeous room you've got here.'

Kate nodded. It *was* gorgeous. And she was going to have to sell it. Because she'd married an idiot! She started to sob harder than ever.

Mike looked horrified and dropped down onto the sofa next to her.

'What *is* it, Kate? What's happened? Was it Pierre?!' he demanded again.

'My ex...' she managed to stutter. 'Ex-husband.' She swallowed. 'Well, not yet.'

'I didn't know you were married,' said Mike quietly.

Kate nodded. 'Not for much longer.'

'I know the feeling,' sighed Mike. This made Kate laugh at the same time as another sob burst out of her, and she let out a strange honking sound that caused Stanley to cock his head.

'Here,' said Mike, reaching into his pocket and handing her a pristine cotton hanky. 'It's clean, I promise!'

Kate mopped at her face and swallowed hard.

'So, what did this ex do?' asked Mike.

'Nothing. I... I left him.'

'Right?'

'I wanted the divorce.'

'Okay?'

'He countered it - so he's divorcing me. For desertion.'

'But... that doesn't change anything, does it?' said Mike, desperately trying to piece this puzzle together as fast as possible. 'That's just words on a form!'

'He...' Kate's lip started to tremble again, and she fought with another wave of emotion as it threatened to crash down on her. 'He called me this evening. He's going to take The Sardine from me!'

That was it. That was all she could tell Mike before she was crying so hard that words were no longer possible. She simply dissolved, and every time she tried to get it under control, the thought of having to leave her sanctuary - the one place in the world that she felt safe - set her off again.

At some point, Stanley came closer and plonked himself down directly in front of the two of them, staring at Kate. Every now and then, he placed his paw on Kate's lap, and when he got no response from her, he glanced at Mike as if asking him to do something about the fact that his best friend was still howling.

The third time he did this, Mike reached out and very gently, very carefully, laid his hand on Stanley's head. 'It's okay lad,' he said softly. 'Your mum'll be okay in a minute.'

It took a good ten minutes for Kate to cry herself out, at which point Mike got to his feet and without saying anything, went through to the kitchen and returned in a couple of minutes with two mugs of peppermint tea.

'Here,' he said, handing one to Kate. 'Hope you don't mind, I helped myself.'

'Thanks,' she said with a shuddering sigh. She balanced the mug on the bare arm of the sofa with one hand and stroked Stanley's head with the other. 'What am I going to do, Mike?' she said in a tiny voice.

'First, you're going to get some rest. You're exhausted. And then, when you've had some sleep, you're going to tell me everything, and I'm going to help you.'

'How?' said Kate, leaning her head back and covering her eyes with her hand. She was struggling to fight the waves of drowsiness that were setting in now she'd stopped crying.

'I've just been through this too, remember?' said Mike, carefully placing his mug down on a side table. 'I've got a really good guy who can help you - or at least give you some advice if you'd like it.'

'But you lost your cafes,' she said, her exhaustion making her blunt and unfiltered.

'Yes - but I got to keep Sarah. And that's what I was

fighting for. That was the only thing that mattered to me.'

Kate turned her head to stare at him. How wrong had she been about this guy?

'How about this,' said Mike, 'maybe we can meet up for lunch tomorrow - after you've had a rest and a lazy morning to yourself. I know Sarah would really like to talk to you - she's worried sick about you too. I'll pack us all a picnic and you can choose where to go?'

Kate nodded, her mind instantly going to the lighthouse. 'That sounds great,' she said, 'But - would you be okay with Stanley coming too?'

'I - oh!'

Mike followed her gaze down to his left hand, which was resting on the big dog's head. He had no idea how long he'd been absentmindedly stroking Stanley's ears.

'Erm,' said Mike. 'Yes. Why not? I think... I think we're friends, aren't we?' He looked back at Kate and their eyes locked. Her hand found his on the sofa, and she squeezed his fingers.

'Yes. I think we are,' she replied.

THE END

Kate and Stanley's story continues with
Trouble in Seabury

ALSO BY BETH RAIN

Seabury Series:

Welcome to Seabury (Seabury Book 1)

Trouble in Seabury (Seabury Book 2)

Christmas in Seabury (Seabury Book 3)

Sandwiches in Seabury (Seabury Book 4)

Secrets in Seabury (Seabury Book 5)

Surprises in Seabury (Seabury Book 6)

Dreams and Ice Creams in Seabury (Seabury Book 7)

Mistakes and Heartbreaks in Seabury (Seabury Book 8)

Laughter and Happy Ever After in Seabury (Seabury Book 9)

A Quiet Life in Seabury (Seabury Book 10)

In A Spin in Seabury (Seabury Book 11)

Living The Dream in Seabury (Seabury Book 12)

A Big Day in Seabury (Seabury Book 13)

Something Borrowed in Seabury (Seabury Book 14)

A Match Made in Seabury (Seabury Book 15)

Seabury Series Collections:

Kate's Story: Books 1 - 3

Hattie's Story: Books 4 - 6

Standalones: Books 7 - 9

Lizzie's Story: Books 10 - 12

Upper Bamton Series:

Upper Bamton: The Complete Series Collection: Books 1 - 4

Individual titles:

A New Arrival in Upper Bamton (Upper Bamton Book 1)

Rainy Days in Upper Bamton (Upper Bamton Book 2)

Hidden Treasures in Upper Bamton (Upper Bamton Book 3)

Time Flies By in Upper Bamton (Upper Bamton Book 4)

Standalone Books:

How to be Angry at Christmas

Crumbleton Series:

Coming Home to Crumbleton (Crumbleton Book 1)

Flowers Go Flying in Crumbleton (Crumbleton Book 2)

Match Point in Crumbleton (Crumbleton Book 3)

A Very Crumbleton Christmas (Crumbleton Book 4)

Little Bamton Series:

Little Bamton: The Complete Series Collection: Books 1 - 5

Individual titles:

Christmas Lights and Snowball Fights (Little Bamton Book 1)

Spring Flowers and April Showers (Little Bamton Book 2)

Summer Nights and Pillow Fights (Little Bamton Book 3)

Autumn Cuddles and Muddy Puddles (Little Bamton Book 4)

Christmas Flings and Wedding Rings (Little Bamton Book 5)

Crumcarey Island Series:

Crumcarey Island Series Collection: Books 1 - 5

Individual titles:

Christmas on Crumcarey (Crumcarey Island Book 1)

All Change on Crumcarey (Crumcarey Island Book 2)

Making Waves on Crumcarey (Crumcarey Island Book 3)

Fool's Gold on Crumcarey (Crumcarey Island Book 4)

A Fresh Start on Crumcarey (Crumcarey Island Book 5)

WRITING AS BEA FOX

What's a Girl To Do? The Complete Series

Individual titles:

The Holiday: What's a Girl To Do? (Book 1)

The Wedding: What's a Girl To Do? (Book 2)

The Lookalike: What's a Girl To Do? (Book 3)

The Reunion: What's a Girl To Do? (Book 4)

At Christmas: What's a Girl To Do? (Book 5)

ABOUT THE AUTHOR

Beth Rain has always wanted to be a writer and has been penning adventures for characters ever since she learned to stare into the middle-distance and daydream.

She recently moved to a windswept, Scottish island, and it is a dream come true to spend her days hanging out with Bob – her trusty laptop – scoffing crisps and chocolate while dreaming up swoony love stories for all her imaginary friends.

Beth's writing will always deliver on the happy-ever-afters, so if you need cosy… you're in safe hands!

Visit www.bethrain.com for all the bookish goodness and keep up with all Beth's news by joining her newsletter!

facebook.com/BethRainBooks
twitter.com/bethrainauthor
instagram.com/bethrainauthor

Printed in Dunstable, United Kingdom